"I enjoy being in charg___

She rested her elbows on the table, fully aware that her sweater slid farther off her shoulder. "I work hard to keep it that way."

He wanted her. From the way he white-knuckled his beer bottle, he wanted her badly. That was very good news.

"What do you do? What are you in charge of?" He took a long swig of beer.

"I'm a systems security analyst."

His eyebrows rose. She wasn't sure, but he looked impressed.

"I know. Computers. It sounds super exciting, doesn't it?" She grinned, leisurely enjoying a second olive.

He shifted in his chair, setting his beer on the table a little harder than necessary.

She bit back a smile. "And you?"

"I'm a cop." He sighed. "A detective."

It took everything she had not to say something about handcuffs. "Really?" She should not be thinking about Patton and his handcuffs.

His eyes narrowed. "You're pretty easy to read."

Cady's cheeks were on fire but she met his gaze. "Then I guess we don't need to worry about foreplay."

Dear Reader,

Cady and Patton's blind date led to something neither one was expecting—a one-night stand that rocks their worlds. But one-night stands are just that, one night. And when their incredible night is over, they go their separate ways and return to their normal lives.

Until Cady's best friend gets engaged to Patton's brother.

Weddings should be happy times. Lots of romance, family and excitement. But Cady and Patton know this engagement is a mistake. One they will work together to stop. If they can keep their hands off each other. And if they can remember that neither one of them believes in romance, falling in love and happy endings.

Writing this story was a delight. Cady is such a strong woman, she knows what she wants and goes for it. Patton is a true alpha, in control in all things. Putting them together and out of their comfort zones led to a supersexy story I sincerely hope you'll enjoy.

I love to hear from readers, so please find me on my website, sashasummers.com, on Facebook, or Twitter, @sashawrites.

Enjoy every page,

Sasha Summers

Sasha Summers

Seducing the Best Man

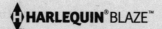

ISBN-13: 978-0-373-79893-3

Seducing the Best Man

Copyright © 2016 by Sasha Best

Printed in U.S.A.

HARLEQUIN®
www.Harlequin.com

Sasha Summers is part gypsy. Her passions have always been storytelling, romance and travel. Whether it's an easy-on-the-eyes cowboy or a hero of mythic proportions, Sasha falls a little in love with each and every one of her heroes. She frequently gets lost with her characters in the world she creates, forgetting those everyday tasks like laundry and dishes. Luckily, her four brilliant children and her hero-inspiring hubby are super understanding and helpful.

Books by Sasha Summers

Harlequin American Romance

The Boones of Texas

A Cowboy's Christmas Reunion
Twins for the Rebel Cowboy

To get the inside scoop on Harlequin Blaze and its talented writers, be sure to check out BlazeAuthors.com.

All backlist available in ebook format.

Visit the Author Profile page at Harlequin.com for more titles.

To the strong women in my life. Stay strong—body, spirit, mind and love.

Acknowledgments
To my daughters, future writers and exceptional brainstorming partners.

Huge thanks to my agent, Pamela Hopkins, for telling me to go for it with this book.

Johanna Raisanen, thanks for giving me this opportunity and your support. And Kathleen Scheibling, thanks for helping me find a yummy drink with olives.

1

CADY WAS GLAD she was running late. It gave her time to recover from the hotter-than-hell man sitting at the table across the restaurant, waiting for her. Bianca had said he was good-looking. *Good*-looking? She and Bianca needed to have a serious talk. This man was meant for getting naked and savoring long lazy days in bed. Or long, sleepless nights in bed…in the shower…on the couch…in the car.

She trailed behind the server to the table, giving herself time to appreciate her date. Broad shoulders. Strong jaw with just the right amount of stubble. Black hair. "Patton?" she held her hand out, unable to deny the slight purr in her voice.

His pale eyes were unexpected beneath his thick eyebrows and inky-black hair. But, pow, they packed a punch—and left a not-so-subtle fire pulsing through her veins.

He stood, towering over her five-foot-two-inch frame. "Cady?"

She nodded, arching a brow. "Guilty." Her brain was filled with all sorts of delectable possibilities.

The corner of his mouth cocked up, and he took her hand in his, shaking it once. His hand was rough, warm and huge. His fingers wrapped around hers, strong but controlled. She couldn't help but wonder how they'd feel on her body, uncontrolled.

She sat, tucking a strand of hair behind her ear. "Sorry to keep you waiting," she said, smiling at him.

He didn't smile back. "No problem," he murmured, sitting across from her.

"Good evening, I'll be your server this evening," their waiter gushed. She took the offered menu, using the opportunity to subtly assess the delicious surprise that was her date.

A quick glance told her he was doing the same thing. But, unlike her, he wasn't trying to be subtle about it. He was staring; his pale blue eyes inspected her with a meticulousness that bordered on rudeness.

"We have a lovely house red this evening," the server offered enthusiastically.

"I'd like a Whiskey Special, extra olives." She smiled up at their server and he smiled back. *He* was good-looking. If Bianca were here, she could explain the difference to her. Questionable manners or not, her date was in another class altogether.

"I'll have a beer." Patton's voice was all gravel and rasp, sending delightful shivers along her spine.

Cady looked at Patton and tucked the same strand of hair behind her ear.

The server excused himself and left them with the menus.

"Who did this to you?" she asked, scanning the menu without looking up.

"What?" he asked, clearly confused by her question.

"Who set you up?" She looked at him, grinning. "Friend or family?"

He gave her a lopsided grin in return. "Family." His gaze held hers. "You?"

"Friend."

His gaze wandered along her neck to the shoulder peeking out of her black sweater. "More pressure that way."

"Really?" Why did it feel as though he was touching her? She shivered.

"You're stuck with family." His eyes returned to her face. "Friends are optional."

"Ouch," she laughed. "Not this one, not really."

He sat the menu aside, but his steely gaze never left her face. She stared right back, exploring the strong jaw and razor-sharp features. He wasn't pretty-boy-handsome, he was…overwhelming.

"Know what you want?"

He smiled—revealing a dimple. "For dinner?"

She was going to need a cold shower soon. "Isn't that what we're talking about?" She swallowed.

"Sure." He sat back in his chair, resting one hand on the table. He stared at her shoulder again.

She cocked her head. "A man of many words."

He shrugged, the lopsided grin returning.

"Conversation helps with things like first dates." She sat forward. "I'll start. Let me guess, you're getting a steak?"

He nodded.

The server delivered their drinks. "Ready to order?"

"Steak, medium rare, baked potato and house salad." Patton handed the menu to their server. He may be hot, but he definitely needed to work on his manners.

"And for the lady?"

Cady smiled up at their server. "I'm not sure—"

"I can come back when you're ready." Their server glanced between them.

"No, no. I hate to keep a man waiting." She took a sip of her drink. "I'll have what the gentleman's having."

"Very good." The server took their menus, shot her another smile and left.

Patton's fingers tapped the table—as if he was distracted or restless. She watched the slight narrowing of his eyes, the occasional twitch of his jaw, the thinning of his lips as he assessed each and every person in the room. He surprised her when he said, "If you weren't ready, you could have said so."

"Or you could have asked." She took another sip of her drink.

Patton's eyes pinned her, the raw intensity in their depths searing her cheeks. His nod was slight, hardly perceptible. His jaw tightened as his entire focus centered on her mouth. She might just be willing to excuse his bad manners.

Who knew a blind date could turn out so…interesting? Bianca had tried to set her up before, determined to help her find Mr. Right. She didn't get Cady's satisfaction with Mr. Right Now. And the men she'd set her up with…it never went well. So when Bianca promised this would be her last attempt *ever*, Cady had agreed. She had no expectations tonight, except dinner. But now… she couldn't remember ever feeling such a raw, instant attraction to a man. All sorts of tingle-inducing expectations were forming.

Her phone vibrated.

After a month of troubleshooting into the wee hours

of the morning, she should have known it was too much to ask for a night to herself. But she'd been saddled with Charles, the boss's son, who couldn't go to the bathroom without consulting her first. If she wanted a promotion and all the trappings that came with it, she had to deal with Charles's crappy program debugs and shoddy work ethic. She pulled her phone from her pocket and sat it on the table. "Excuse me," she murmured, reading the message.

"Everything okay?"

"Ever feel like you're the only one that knows what they're doing?" she asked, answering the text.

"Every day," he answered.

She paused midtext and glanced at him. "It's exhausting, isn't it?" Was he looking at her hands? Her wrists?

"But necessary—if you want things to get done right," his voice rumbled.

She ignored the thrill that rumble elicited, hit Send and slid the phone aside. "Exactly." Maybe they did have something in common...

"Work?" he asked, motioning at her phone with the beer bottle in his hand.

She nodded.

He glanced at his watch. "You keep odd hours?"

"I guess. But my job is time-sensitive, so if I get a text, I answer it."

"You enjoy that? Being on call?"

She knew he was watching her as she lifted the olive-laden toothpick to her mouth and pulled one off with her teeth. But she didn't answer until she'd swallowed the olive and taken a sip of her drink. "I enjoy being in charge." She rested her elbows on the table, fully aware that her sweater slid farther off her shoulder. Fully aware that he was staring at her shoulder. She liked the way his jaw clenched. She liked the way her body tightened, yearning for this man. Her voice was a little husky when she added, "I work hard to keep it that way."

His gaze slammed into hers, knocking the air from her lungs. He wanted her. From the way he white-knuckled his beer bottle, he wanted her badly. That was very good news.

"What do you do? What are you in charge of?" He took a long swig of beer.

"For work?"

"Isn't that what we're talking about?" He cocked an eyebrow, leveling her with a lethal, crooked grin.

"Sure," she teased. "I'm a systems security analyst."

His eyebrows rose. She wasn't sure, but he looked impressed.

"I know. Computers. It sounds super exciting, doesn't it?" She grinned, leisurely enjoying a second olive.

He shifted in his chair, setting his beer on the table a little harder than necessary.

She bit back a smile. "And you?"

"I'm a cop." He sighed. "A detective."

It took everything she had not to say something about handcuffs. She really wanted to. "Really?" She should not be thinking about Patton and his handcuffs. Oh hell, there was no way she could stop thinking about Patton and handcuffs.

His eyes narrowed, the muscle in his cheek jumping. "You're pretty easy to read."

Cady's cheeks were on fire but she met his gaze. "Then I guess we don't need to worry about foreplay."

HE KNEW AN invitation when he heard one. His body accepted. But he'd be damned if he let his dick make his mind up for him tonight. He tore his gaze from hers, on the verge of exploding. His one-night-stand days were over; he'd outgrown the thrill of the hunt years ago. But *if* he did, she would be impossible to resist.

Focusing on something else—anything else—was impossible. She was the sexiest thing he'd ever laid eyes on. Petite, feminine and a whole lot of fire. Sleek auburn hair, cut short along her jawline, interrupted by a bold stripe of blond. He didn't like short hair on a woman, but he couldn't deny there was something very appealing about Cady's slender neck. Every damn time she tucked the blond strand of hair behind her ear, he imagined sucking on her ear lobe. And her shoulder… His hand itched to slip inside the neck of her low-hanging sweater. He wanted the weight of her breast in his hand. He wanted to touch her, to taste her.

What the hell was wrong with him? After working three days straight, he'd wanted to go home, walk the dog, watch some sports, nuke his dinner and sleep for a good ten hours.

His family was worried about him, he knew that. They all wanted him to get out and live a little—let go of what happened. This blind date was his brother Zach's idea. A date that wasn't supposed to happen, but he'd forgotten to cancel. Now, Patton couldn't decide whether he wanted to thank his brother, or knock his lights out. There was no way Zach could know how Cady would affect him, but still… Looking at Cady, tonight he really did want to "live a little."

Her fingernails were dark blue, a stark contrast to her pale skin. He watched her small, agile fingers stir the olive-skewered toothpick in her drink. If she used her little pink tongue on one more damn olive, he was going to break something. Her huge brown eyes fixed on her drink. And her mouth... He took another long pull of his beer. Her lips were full and red and meant for tasting.

"See anything you like?" She looked at him, peeking up at him through long lashes.

Her words were soft, not nearly as cocky as she meant them to be. But he liked the softness, the hint of uncertainty. It was the hesitancy that made him answer honestly, "Yes."

She blinked, those full red lips parting.

"I have your salads." Their salads were placed on the table. "Pepper?"

Patton shook his head. Their pretty-boy waiter and his pepper grinder needed to back the hell away from the table.

"No, thank you," Cady added, her eyes never wavering from his.

"Another round?" the waiter asked, disappearing at their nod.

"What am I thinking?" Cady asked Patton, her hands loosely resting on either side of her drink.

He shook his head. He didn't miss the shudder that ran along that bare shoulder or the way her breathing had picked up. The slight flush creeping along her skin told him everything—she was just as worked up as he was.

"Don't know or won't say?"

"Maybe I'll show you later," he murmured, fascinated by the way her eyes closed briefly and she bit her lower lip.

Her brown eyes were molten, exploring his face. "I'm not that hungry—"

"You will be," he argued.

She picked up her toothpick, the olive heading for her mouth. A bolt of hunger tightened his already rock-hard erection. His hand encircled her wrist, stopping her. He couldn't be held responsible for his actions if she ate that damn olive.

"Not a fan of olives?" she asked.

"Not at the moment." His fingers slid along her forearm, tracing the slight indention at her elbow. He pulled his hand back, the feel of her satin skin still on the tips of his fingers. How long had it been since he'd wanted to touch someone? To feel something? Right now, he'd never wanted anything more. He flexed his hand then gripped the empty beer bottle.

Her phone vibrated again, immediately grabbing her attention. She relaxed, transformed from sexy to sweet by the all-encompassing smile on her face. "It's Bibi," she said.

"Bibi?"

"The one who set this up." She tucked that piece of hair behind her ear again, unknowingly taunting him. "She told me to behave." Her brown eyes met his.

"What are you telling her?"

"Not likely," she murmured, her voice breathy.

"Here you go." The waiter placed their drinks on the table. "Your steaks will be out shortly."

There was no mistaking the desire in her eyes as she rasped, "Can we get that to go?"

Patton's pants grew painfully tight.

"To go?" the waiter asked.

"To go," Patton affirmed. The sooner the better. At

the moment, he was seriously contemplating breaking a few laws about what should or shouldn't be done in public. It was crazy, he knew it, but he didn't care.

"Of course." The look of confusion on the waiter's face as he left was comical.

"Unless you have plans?" she said with a coy grin. "I thought I'd be going to bed early tonight."

"Oh, you are." He couldn't resist, or hold back the smile.

She laughed. "You're a surprise, Patton."

He was a surprise? He shook his head.

Their waiter returned long enough to place their to-go bag on the table, setting the small black bill binder on the table. "It was a pleasure serving you this evening."

Patton pulled his wallet out, tucked several bills in the binder and stood. He came around the table and slid Cady's chair back for her.

Cady stared up at him. "I knew you had it in you to be a gentleman." She stood, leaning closer and lowering her voice. "I'm not really looking for a gentleman tonight."

Patton stared down at her. "Good to know." The few inches between them was charged with undiluted hunger. He couldn't resist. His hand cupped her cheek, his thumb tracing the fullness of her lower lip. The simple touch had her leaning into his hand and him leaning into her. When her lips fastened on his thumb, his breath escaped on a hiss. She smiled up at him, the thrill of power in her gaze a challenge he'd gladly accept.

He took her hand and led her from the restaurant. He had no idea where they were going. It would take too long to get to his place, and he didn't want to wait.

Once they were outside the restaurant, he sized up their options. They were downtown, a place he tended to avoid. But there were perks. Like having two hotels to choose from within walking distance. He picked the closer, heading in that direction. Her fingers twined with his, inflaming and soothing him. He glanced at her, taking in her flushed cheeks and accelerated breathing. She felt it, too.

It took ten minutes to check in to the upscale hotel.

He took the key card, and Cady tugged him into the elevator. He waited until the doors closed behind them before grabbing her around the waist and lifting her to sit on the wooden railing that lined the elevator.

She reached for him, threading her fingers in his hair. "Kiss me." It was part plea, part demand—the hitch in her voice telling him everything he needed to know. She wasn't as in control as she pretended to be.

Neither was he.

He bent his head and her fingers tightened in his hair, pulling him close. He angled his head, dragging his nose along the shell of her ear and the arch of her neck. Her scent wrapped around him, drawing him to her. He tilted her head back, his mouth grazing her skin where neck met shoulder. She shivered, her skin contracting beneath his lips.

The elevator dinged, forcing them apart. He helped her from the rail before an older couple and several teenagers joined them. She stood in front of him, the curve of her hip resting against the ridged length of his arousal. His hand skimmed along her hip then slid around her waist to rest against the lower part of her stomach. He could feel each unsteady breath.

The ride to the eighth floor took too freaking long.

The elevator dinged, and Cady pulled him from the elevator. She turned into him, knocking them into the wall as she stood on tiptoe to kiss him. He caught her, his hand cradling the back of her head. Her lips were soft, welcoming him, opening to him. Her breath, her tongue... When his hand slipped to the bare skin of her shoulder, he couldn't stop his groan from spilling out into the hallway.

The elevator dinged again behind them, reminding him that they still hadn't reached their destination. He read the small room number plaque, gripped Cady's hand and led her to their room. She opened the door and he kicked it shut behind her.

She pulled off her sweater, wriggling out of her gray skirt and heels before he'd caught his breath. And seeing her, in barely-there black panties and a bra that left little to the imagination, knocked the breath out of him again.

He shook his head. "Cady—"

She launched herself at him, pressing those silky curves against his still-dressed chest. He didn't argue when her hands tore open his shirt, sending buttons flying all over the room. He didn't give his scars a second thought as he yanked off his undershirt; shedding clothes was the only thing that mattered. He wanted to feel all of her against all of him.

His mouth devoured hers, nipping her lower lip, sucking it into his mouth and sealing them together. She swayed into him but he held her up. He couldn't get enough of her, deepening the kiss until he was dizzy with the taste of her.

They stumbled across the room to the massive bed, hands and mouths exploring. She lay back on the bed, breathing hard.

"You're beautiful," he rasped, meaning it.

She rested on her elbows, staring up at him. "So are you, Patton." She sat up then, her fingers trailing down his shoulders. She paused at the sight of the scars, but not for long. Then her fingers were stroking down his chest, to his stomach. She tugged his boxer briefs down and smiled, falling back onto her elbows again. "This night just gets better and better."

He choked on his laughter when those dark-blue-tipped fingers wrapped around his cock.

"Wow," she whispered.

He knelt, tugging her panties off and throwing them over his shoulder. She watched as his hands explored the dip of her hip, the curve of her thigh, the soft thatch of hair between her legs. Her legs parted for him and he stared up at her. She had no inhibition… And it was sexy as hell. He kissed her stomach, licking her belly button while his hands ran back up her stomach to the satin of her bra.

"Patton," she whispered. "Please." She buried her hands in his hair, tugging him up.

His arm held her to the bed as his tongue found the soft nub at her core. Her hands gripped his hair, her moan soft and breathy. He smiled, using the tip of his tongue to set a quick, light rhythm. She tried to arch up, to move, but his arm kept her still. His tongue continued as he slipped a finger deep inside her. Hand and mouth, he fought his own desire until her hands fisted in his hair, her body bowed off the bed and a raw moan tore from her throat. It took everything he had not to bury himself inside her then, but he wasn't done yet.

He kissed his way up her body, lingering over the ridge of her hip and the underside of her breast. He tugged the lacy cups down so his tongue could explore the tight peaks of her breasts, sucking first one nipple, then the other.

He settled between her thighs, so hard it hurt. "I don't have any protection—"

"I'm protected." She paused and took a deep, shaky breath. "I'm clean. Are you?"

He nodded, holding her gaze. She reached for him, gripping his upper arms and hooking one leg around his hips. His breath hitched as he pressed into her slowly. She was so hot, so tight. He closed his eyes briefly, reining in the need to move. But he wanted to see her, to watch her. Her lips parted, her eyes closed. Her hands gripped his forearms tightly, and her head lifted off the bed.

Her hands moved, clasping his hips. "Please." Her nails dug in.

He eased into her, letting her adjust to him. But when she started to move, he decided to let her take charge—he wanted to watch her. He rolled them, pulling her on top.

She smiled down at him, running her hands across his face and along his shoulders. She braced herself on his chest and began to move. Her back arched, her breasts swaying in time. His hands slid up her sides, cupping her breasts, teasing the nipples that peaked over the lacy cups of her bra. He loved the way she felt, the sounds she made. He pressed kisses to her side and nuzzled the place between her breasts, drawing her scent in.

Her movements grew frenzied, out of control. Her hands moved over his chest, her nails raking across his skin. Each touch, every thrust, pushed him closer. But he held on until her body clenched around him. She cried out, her climax forcing his release. He gripped her hips, holding her tightly against him as his orgasm ripped through him. He couldn't stop his groan, or ease his hold on her.

She collapsed on his chest, gasping for breath. He stroked the length of her back, his fingers tracing each notch of her spine. She was soft and warm, so he wrapped his arms around her and lay there. He didn't know what the hell he was doing, but it felt good. It was the first time—in a long time—that the ache in his heart and the scars on his chest didn't keep him from falling into a deep, restful sleep.

2

"THE GOOD CHINA?" Patton eyed his mother's carefully set table.

"Zach said he had big news." His mother sounded far too excited.

Patton knew his mother. He also knew his brother Zach. The two of them had a bond he and his other brother Spence didn't understand. "You have any idea what his big news is?"

His mother glanced at him, her light blue eyes bright. "No."

He arched an eyebrow.

"I don't," she argued. "Don't you use that look on your mother."

He smiled. "It normally gets me results."

She put her hands on her hips. "Only if someone has something to hide. I don't."

He held up his hands. "Okay, fine."

"She tell you what's going on?" Spence arrived, carrying a bag of ice. "Whoa, the good china?"

Patton nodded. "Exactly."

"You two knock it off." Imogene Ryan shooed her

sons out of the way and headed to the kitchen, still talking. "A woman has a right to make things pretty every once in a while—for no apparent reason. I'm not getting any younger, you know. I don't see the harm in setting a nice table once a month instead of three times a year."

"Who got her all worked up?" Spence asked softly.

Patton shrugged. "I just asked her if she knew what the news was—"

"And I don't," their mother called from the kitchen.

Spence laughed and Patton shook his head. She'd always had ridiculously good hearing. It had made sneaking out of the house almost impossible as teenagers. Almost.

"We're here," Zach's voice came from the front door.

"We?" Spence asked.

Patton shrugged, following Spence into the front sitting room. Their mother brushed past them both, making Patton the last one into the room. His younger brother Zach was holding a bouquet of flowers in one hand and the hand of a very pretty young woman with the other.

"Mom, this is Bianca." Zach was smiling. But it was the way he was smiling that drew Patton up short. His little brother was smiling like a kid in a candy shop with an unlimited budget. "Bianca, this is my mother, Imogene Ryan."

Patton glanced at the young woman on his arm. His brother was clearly smitten, not that this was necessarily new. Zach was always getting a new girlfriend—his problem seemed to be keeping them. Then again, Zach had never brought one home before, so this would be interesting.

"Mrs. Ryan, it's so lovely to meet you." Bianca's voice wavered—she was nervous.

"Oh, Bianca, please, call me Imogene." His mother pulled Bianca into a hug. "Zach's told me so much about you."

Patton shot Spence a look. Spence shook his head, shrugging in answer. Apparently their mother was the only one who had heard about Bianca. Not that he and his brothers talked daily, but the family still had dinner together once a week. It seemed a little odd that Bianca had never come up in conversation.

"I figured it's time for her to meet the family now that she's agreed to marry me." Zach's voice was unsteady, his eyes bouncing between the three waiting members of his family.

Patton blew out a deep breath, stunned by the announcement.

Their mother was clapping her hands, hugging Bianca again then Zach. She chattered away, her excitement covering for his complete shock. Spence seemed to snap out of it, too. He exchanged an awkward handshake then a one-armed hug with Bianca before tackling Zach.

When both his mother and Bianca were staring at him, he pulled it together and stepped forward. "Nice to meet you," he murmured, shaking her hand. "I'm Patton. And...welcome to the family."

Bianca smiled, her tawny eyes wide. "You, too. I mean, it's nice to meet you."

"Let's celebrate!" His mother was still on a visible high. "I made some fresh-squeezed lemonade and cookies—"

"I'll get it," Patton volunteered, heading into the kitchen.

A tray with the "fancy" crystal goblets and a plate of homemade wedding cookies waited. He eyed the cookies. His mother might not have known Zach had proposed, but she knew something was going on. Not that this surprised him. She normally knew what was happening before anyone else did. She was a born investigator and a master at deductive reasoning.

He shook his head and opened the refrigerator. His search for the pitcher of lemonade was derailed by a bottle full of olives. Green olives. An instant flash of Cady's lips, her pearly white teeth tugging the skewered olive off the toothpick and into her mouth. He closed his eyes, his grip on the refrigerator door tightening. It wasn't the first time in the last two weeks he'd been caught up in the memory of that night. Something about Cady had latched on to him tightly. It didn't take much to stir the echo of her touch, the warmth of her body, the husky timbre of her sigh as if she was standing before him—staring at him with that saucy grin of hers.

He'd woken up in that hotel room, drained but exhilarated. He didn't know what he'd expected, but it hadn't been an empty bed. She had been gone, but the all-consuming hunger hadn't. He'd found himself thinking about her at work, while walking his dog, Mikey, and right before he fell into a restless sleep. Why he couldn't get her out of his mind, he didn't know. It was a damn good thing he didn't know her last name, or he'd have tried to track her down by now. And that have would be bad, for both of them. Clearly, Cady was dangerous…an addiction in the making. He'd made a mistake, giving in to her. He knew better. He didn't have time for distractions, not now. Not ever. He'd had enough of heartache in his life. When his father was alive and on the force, it had been Patton's job to comfort his mother through hours of grief and worry. The thought of someone who cared about him going through that… Nope, he was just fine staying a bachelor—without complication or distraction.

Spence was at his side, staring into the open refrigerator. "It's right there." His brother pulled the pitcher from the refrigerator. He shot him a look. "What's eating you?"

Patton sighed, pushing thoughts of Cady from his mind and the door shut. "Long week."

"Every week's a long week," Spence said. "Doesn't mean you need to let all the penguins out." He nodded at the now-closed fridge. "You okay?"

Patton nodded. "Surprised."

"That's for sure," Spence agreed. "But as long as Zach's happy."

Patton didn't respond to that. Happiness was a fickle emotion. Especially when it revolved around another person. Sure, he wanted his brothers loved and cared for, but this was way too fast—especially with his little brother's track record. "How long has he known her?"

Spence put the pitcher on the tray. "A month."

Patton shook his head.

"Don't get all cynical. Give her a chance." He lifted the tray. "Mom's a pretty good judge of character—"

"Spence, Zach's talking about getting married to this girl. Marriage leads to kids." Patton's grin was reluctant. "Which has been Mom's constant birthday and holiday wish for the past eight years. I'm thinking her judgment might be a little skewed this time."

"Maybe." Spence laughed, carrying the tray out. "But you might as well get over it and come get acquainted with your sister-in-law-to-be."

Patton glared at the door. Zach was the golden boy, the only non-cop amongst them. Zach made more money than both Spence and Patton combined, racking up airline points and traveling on the fly. While Patton admired his little brother's willingness to think outside the box and work hard to get what he wanted, his brother was also a player. He and Spence had been regaled with far too many of their little brother's romantic exploits for Patton to buy into this sudden commitment. Not Zach's normal MO. If this whole engagement fiasco went the way he suspected, a lot of people would wind up hurt.

He pushed through the kitchen door and joined the others in the sitting room to find conversation in full swing.

"What are we talking about?" Patton asked.

"Flowers," Zach offered. "Bianca has a flower shop. That's where we met," he paused, squeezing Bianca's hand. "She helped me put an arrangement together."

"You own your own shop?" Patton asked.

"Bianca's Jardin?" She smiled. "It's small. On the corner of Hazelwood and Main—in Lassiter. It's also a tearoom. Just high tea, a few days a week, but my cousin Celeste handles that part of it."

He glanced back and forth between Bianca and Zach, asking, "You two met a month ago?"

Zach shot him a look.

Patton cocked an eyebrow.

"I can't believe it's only been a month." Bianca's voice trembled.

"Feels like we've known each other for a lot longer," Zach murmured, smiling at Bianca. And Bianca beamed back at him.

Patton popped a wedding cookie into his mouth to keep from snorting. He swallowed, adding, "Nothing wrong with a long engagement."

"Who said anything about a long engagement?" Zach asked before biting a cookie.

His mother hopped up. "Oh, Patton, shush. There's no time like the present. I'm going to call Henrietta and see if Tucker House has an opening for an engagement shindig."

Bianca looked stunned. "Oh Imogene, you do not need to—"

"I want to, darling," his mother cut her off, smiling from ear to ear. "Patton might be a stick in the mud, but I know how precious time is. We're not putting a thing off. We're celebrating every second."

The way Zach was looking at Bianca made him wonder, for a second, if his brother was actually in love. Maybe it was more than attraction. Maybe... Doubtful. He sipped his lemonade, smiling pleasantly at Bianca when she glanced his way. As much as he'd like to be wrong, he knew there was no way someone could fall in love in a month. Not the kind of love that would last forever— He doubted that kind of love existed. His engagement to Ellie—someone he'd known most of his life—had ended with the first obstacle they'd faced. And now he worried his little brother's new crush might end up having lasting consequences for them all.

"What do you mean you're getting married?" Cady's heart was lodged in her throat. "Bianca, you can't be serious." She knew Bianca. She knew how focused her friend was. Bianca was careful, methodical—she'd set a goal and she wouldn't let anything get in her way.

Bianca laughed. "I'm totally serious. You met him. Zach?"

Cady remembered him all right. Zach. The good-looking, charming one that was far too proprietary over her best friend. "The controlling, handsome one?"

"Controlling?" Bianca's eyes went round.

"Controlling." Cady sat forward. "Why marriage? Can't you just bang his brains out for a while? Get him out of your system."

Bianca frowned. "Cady."

"Don't Cady me, girl." Cady sighed. "Why? Are you knocked up?"

"No!" Bianca cried, glaring her disapproval. "I'm marrying him because I love him." Bianca's simple answer made Cady wrinkle up her nose.

"Oh, please." She shifted in her wrought-iron chair, staring blindly down the street to the fair at the end of the block. She and Bianca had come here the past few years, enjoying the wine tasting, touring the historic homes and exploring the booths of handmade treats and crafts. It was their thing—something that would change if Bianca got married. And while Bianca's idea of marriage had always been warm and fuzzy and complete fiction, Cady knew the truth. Marriage, love and commitment were illusions. What happened after the honeymoon? Compromise to the point of losing one's self, resentment or disgust replacing affection for your once-dreamy significant other, and—ultimately—betrayal and distrust. Not that Bianca saw it that way.

"His family is throwing us an engagement party Friday," Bianca added, pulling Cady from her thoughts. "Apparently they know the woman who owns one of the inns on the lake."

Cady stared at Bianca. "Friday as in two days?"

Bianca nodded. "You have to come."

Cady frowned. "What does Zach do?"

"He's a promoter for a luxury resort chain. He just loves it. They have locations all over the world that he gets to visit. And they're growing."

"While he's off traveling the world, you'll stay here?" Cady asked, frowning.

Bianca shrugged.

"Well, you can't travel all the time," Cady pointed out. "What about the shop?"

Bianca's answer was soft, "We haven't worked out all the details yet."

"Details of your everyday life? Don't you think you should do that before making him fifty percent owner in your shop? Texas is a fifty-fifty state, Bibi." She took a deep breath. "You love your shop. You've fought tooth and nail to buy that space, to open your own business. Since the day we met, you've talked about this. Having a shop like the one your grandfather had in Puerto Rico."

"Cady," Bianca sighed. "Zach is willing to take a demotion so he doesn't have to travel."

"You don't think he'd come to resent you for that later?" Cady shook her head. "I know you, Bibi. If there's a compromise to be made, you're the one who'll end up making it."

Bianca shook her head. "We'll find a way to make it work without sacrificing our personal dreams along the way." Bianca paused, stirring her iced tea with a long spoon. "The shop wasn't my only dream, Cady. You know that."

Cady did know. Bianca was the earth-mother type. Cady fought to convince her that kids, the minivan, the Saturday soccer games, big birthday parties and the adoring husbands would never be as rewarding as a solid career and loyal friendships. Bianca didn't buy it. Even after having her heart ground to bits, Bianca held on to the hope that she'd find real love and support in the form of her own personal Prince Charming.

"Shack up with the guy," Cady argued. "Why do you need to marry this Zach?"

Bianca laughed. "My family would love that."

"They're okay with you marrying some guy you've known for five minutes?"

Bianca frowned at her. "It's been longer than that."

Cady shot her a disbelieving look. "Fine, five hours."

"I love him, Cady. I see a future with him. One I want." She stared into her iced tea. "It would mean a lot if you could support me."

Bianca was serious. Dead serious. And Cady didn't know what to do. Since freshman year of college, the two of them had been through a lot. They didn't have much in common, but somehow that didn't matter. Bianca had grown up in a huge, sometimes too invasive family of unwavering loyalty and strong opinions— freely shared. While Cady's childhood was comprised of disappointing birthdays, indifferent and cold holidays, and broken promises. Over the years, Bianca had been a conscience when Cady needed it. And Cady had been the realist when Bianca needed it. Apparently, that wasn't right now, no matter what Cady thought.

"I love you, Bibi." Cady took her friend's hand in

hers. "I'm not a good liar, you know that, so I can't gush and jump up and down over this, okay? But I'll try to wrap my head around this for you."

Bianca smiled. "I really appreciate it, Cady. Give him a chance. I know you'll become good friends."

Cady shrugged. She didn't want to be good friends with him. She liked things the way they were. Adding a man to this equation made her a third wheel.

"I'll be back, nature calls." Bianca left their café table and headed inside.

Cady sighed, taking the last sip of her drink. She picked up the last olive and stared at it, turning the toothpick in her fingers. She could almost feel Patton's pale blue eyes, staring down at her, jaw locked as his arms braced him over her. Feel the muscles along his sides beneath her hands rippling as he moved into her. She shuddered, dropping the olive into her empty glass.

She blinked, staring down the street at the crowds milling about. Patton had been a mistake. He was the sort of man a girl didn't forget. He was the sort she spent the rest of her life comparing her bedmates to. He'd made her feel sexy and beautiful—and he'd left an ache inside her she was having a hard time ignoring.

She'd crept out of that bed as quietly as possible. She always made sure never to be the one waking up in an empty bed: it was an ego thing really. But after such an amazing night, she couldn't risk it. She'd glanced at Patton as she retrieved her clothing from under the bed, the top of the dresser, the bathroom floor and one of the lampshades. If he'd woken up, she would have gladly gone for another round. But he hadn't woken up. Normally, she didn't linger or have to force herself to leave. But their night together had been anything but normal.

In the end she'd left—torn. And his memory remained. She picked up the olive, spinning it in her fingers. How could she still ache for the burn of his touch, for him?

"Cady?" Bianca sat down. "What's the matter? You've been so preoccupied recently. Maybe you have someone special in your life you're keeping a secret?"

Cady drew in a deep breath. She wasn't going to tell Bianca about Patton. When she'd asked how the date went, Cady told her there wasn't much to tell. She'd said that she and Patton had had a little conversation and parted ways. Which was mostly true. Why she didn't want to talk about him—to share him or that night—was a mystery. Normally, she told Bianca everything, no matter how shocking. But this time was different. She still wanted Patton. So it was best not to think about him or his piercing eyes. Or the way his breath felt on her stomach. Or his fingers along her side, gripping her hip. She swallowed. So much for not thinking about him.

Every time she saw a broad set of shoulders and thick, unruly black hair, she was gripped with a knot of anticipation so strong she could barely move.

"No." Cady shook her head. "Nobody special. Work. And since I have to go to your engagement party Friday night, I can't go trawling for a good time." Which was a shame because the best way to get over Patton was to replace him.

Bianca shook her head. "I worry about you."

Cady waved her away. "Don't worry about me. I don't want to give you wrinkles." She winked. "So, I'm guessing his family is happy? Since this party is happening."

Bianca nodded. "It's his mother mostly, a delightful woman. So sweet."

"And Zach's father?"

"Mr. Ryan died a couple of years ago, a heart attack I think." She shrugged. "Zach said he was under constant stress, the all-work no-play sort." She looked meaningfully at Cady.

"Oh, honey, I play." She smiled sweetly back.

Bianca giggled. "That's not what I meant and you know it."

Cady laughed, too.

"I'm nervous," Bianca sighed. "I want to make a good impression on his family, his colleagues and his friends."

"Oh, Bibi. All a person has to do is look at you to know you're a gem. If anything, you'd better hope the Garzas accept *him*." Cady shook her head. She'd only met the guy once, but Zach Ryan was going to have to prove he was worthy of Bibi. And it wouldn't be easy. Bianca had been down this road before, and it hadn't ended well. Maybe that was why Cady was so resistant? She didn't want to see her best friend hurt again. "I just can't believe this is happening." She barely kept her panic at bay.

"I know. Isn't it wonderful?" Bianca's smile was huge. "And, Cady, GG had a dream. A good dream about me and Zach."

Which clinched it. The women in Bianca's family were matchmakers. If they had a dream about a couple, it was a done deal. But a dream didn't ease Cady's worry. She couldn't give this engagement her approval until she got to know Zach Ryan, his motives and what he had to offer Bianca.

CADY PUT HER sleek little sports car in park and smiled her thanks at the valet who opened her door. She handed over the keys and strode up the steps leading into Tucker House. She paused long enough to take in the spectacular view of the lake. A row of small cabanas, a few beach umbrellas and chairs, illuminated with tiki torches and scattered fire pits. All in all, it was an inviting venue. Even though she had no desire to be here. She smoothed the halter tie of her emerald cocktail dress, made sure her strappy heels were secure, tucked her hair behind her ear and pushed through the door to find the party in full swing.

A few faces were familiar, making it easy to chat her way across the crowded rooms until she'd found Bianca's grandmother. Cady loved Bianca's grandmother, known as GG to those closest to her. The woman was no-nonsense, fiercely independent and unflinchingly loyal to her family. Cady was truly blessed to have been unofficially adopted by the Garza matriarch and the Garza family.

"You look ravishing, GG." Cady hugged the petite woman.

"You are too kind, Cady." She patted Cady's arm. "Now go find Bianca and talk some sense into her."

Cady stared down at the woman. The music, classic big band, was a little loud, so maybe she'd misheard. "Sense?" So GG was on the same page as Cady? If that was the case, this wedding was doomed.

"She is dancing." GG moaned. "In heels. Heels?"

Cady laughed then. Bianca was not the most graceful of girls. She had a trick ankle that gave out all the time. Wearing heels was never a good idea. But dancing in them? "Maybe Zach is a great dancer?"

GG pointed. "I left. I couldn't bear to watch anymore."

"Want me to go check?" Cady asked, glancing in the direction of the music.

"Yes, please." GG patted her again. "And bring me some champagne on your way back."

Cady grinned. "Okay."

She crossed the room, smiling her dazzling smile at the gentleman ogling her from the corner. Maybe she'd get lucky after all? If she could find someone to help her stop thinking about Patton, the night wouldn't be a total loss… The woman next to him—his wife perhaps—intercepted his look and scowled. Cady didn't envy him the set down he was getting. Another reason commitment didn't appeal to her. She didn't belong to anyone and had no desire to.

By the time she'd reached the dance floor, she was more relaxed. If nothing else, the music was good and the drinks were plentiful. She could do this, she could get through tonight—for Bibi. And keep a close eye on Zach Ryan in the process.

The band was playing "In the Mood" and, from the smile on her face, Bianca was having the time of her life. Zach was swinging her all over the place, making it look easy. One perk, he could dance. She zeroed in on him, assessing every inch of him.

Two perks then. Zach Ryan was very attractive. But that didn't mean he was husband material for Bibi.

Her elbow was bumped, jostling her attention. A small crowd had gathered, watching the spin and twirl around the dance floor. Bibi was flushed and bright eyed—there was no denying her near-blissful state. She couldn't help but smile—along with everyone else lining the dance floor—as Bianca laughed out loud…

Wait a minute, she frowned, ratcheting down her emotions. It was a party. People laughed at parties. Just because they danced well together didn't mean they were a good couple. She'd have to get over all the doe eyes and blushing to figure out if this guy was the real deal.

Bianca had a lot on her plate, barely keeping the shop open. A distraction like Zach could be costly. A distraction that could totally destroy Bianca's heart… Cady's heart rate picked up, her anxiety and worry mounting. She had to stay cool, calm and collected. If she went on the immediate offensive, she'd be risking Bianca's friendship, and she couldn't bear the thought of that.

"Champagne?" A server held a silver tray of flutes full of golden bubbles.

She took a glass of champagne from the tray, nodding her thanks at the server, and took a long sip.

That's when she saw him. *Him* him. Patton.

He was completely frozen, staring at her from the other side of the room.

3

PATTON ALMOST BROKE the champagne stem in half. What the hell was she doing here? Now? When his tension was at an all-time high and his patience at an all-time low. Best course of action—avoid her and prevent his total loss of control. She hadn't seen him yet. There was still time. But he couldn't move.

She was mesmerizing, demanding his attention. He swallowed. Her green dress plunged low, revealing too much of the silky soft breasts he remembered so fondly. The skirt skimmed the tops of her knees, showcasing killer calves in mile-high heels. He'd kissed the dip behind her knee, caressed every inch of those legs. And damn, seeing her now, he knew he would to do it again.

When she tipped back her champagne glass, those big brown eyes locked with his. The bolt of recognition, of want, of need, knocked the air from his lungs. Color flooded her cheeks as she tipped her glass in silent salute. But it was her smile that forced him toward her, right as the music stopped. The crowd around the dance floor broke up, milling about and blocking his path. When he looked again, she was gone.

Was he going crazy? It was possible. He sure as hell spent too much time working and too little time sleeping. When he wasn't working, he was walking the dog, skimming books or aimlessly flipping channels. Cady had given him something to think about, something to soothe the ache in his chest. She'd been the first thing to push aside from his mind the accident, his brother Russ's death and the fallout with his father. He'd thought about her a lot—too much. And thinking about her had side effects—like wanting her. Wanting her so bad that long cold showers had cut into his already limited sleep time. Maybe that's why he *saw* her. Because nothing sounded as good as touching her, of losing himself in her. God knows he'd rather be in bed with her right now than be here.

"Guess it's a good thing we had to take dance lessons when we were little?" Spence clapped him on the shoulder.

Patton shook his head, still scanning the room. "I have yet to find a use for them."

"I think you actually have to dance," Spence teased. "Speaking of which, Ellie is here."

"Why?" But Patton knew the answer. Ellie had been his fiancée—for less than two months—four years ago. She couldn't handle his long hours or the danger his job put him in. When his brother Russ died, Ellie had waited a few weeks before quietly breaking it off. He hadn't blamed her. Or been hurt by the breakup. The accident had changed a lot of things. Since Ellie had never become involved with someone else, she must still be pining for Patton. Or so his mother suggested—over and over.

Patton shook his head. "Great." He sighed. No sign

of Ellie. He frowned. He'd been too busy imagining his hot one-night stand to notice Ellie anyway. He was in serious trouble.

"Damn, Patton, Zach might not have noticed your hangdog expression yet, but it's kind of hard to miss." Spence shook his head. "Want a drink?"

He nodded. His brother was right. No matter how he felt about this engagement—or this party—he didn't need to ruin it for everyone.

"Be back." Spence wandered toward the bar.

"Ladies and gents, the buffet is open, so enjoy. We'll be back soon," one of the band members spoke into the mic.

The buffet. One of the many things he'd disapproved of. And renting the Tucker House. And flying in their great aunt and uncle for the weekend. It was an engagement party—not a wedding. If his mother continued to spend big, the wedding might just bankrupt her. He was still frowning when he took in the buffet spread. Only the best for their guests. Shrimp cocktail, canapés, mini quiches, cheese puffs, crab cakes and a make-your-own salad waited. And that was just the appetizers. He closed his eyes, refusing to think about the bills he'd be poring over at the end of the month.

Might as well enjoy it. He loaded his plate up then went in search of a quiet corner.

"Patton." Zach waved him over, Bianca smiling brilliantly at his side.

Patton swallowed his curse and forced himself to smile. He hoped it was a smile, it felt more like a grimace. For the next twenty minutes, he ate his appetizers and attempted to make small talk with his friends and family. He grinned when he should, he answered questions concisely—not rudely—and tried to let go of his restlessness.

"You're the big brother?" Leticia Garza, Bianca's grandmother, asked as she sized him up.

"I am."

"Too bad my Bianca didn't meet you first." She grinned. "Zach is a sweet boy. But you, Mr. Patton, are a man."

Patton couldn't hold back his laugh.

"You should do that more often," Ellie's voice was soft, but Patton recognized it nonetheless. He turned, smiling at the woman he'd once considered marrying. "How are you, Patton?" she asked, leaning forward to press a kiss to his cheek.

Patton returned the kiss, catching a whiff of her sweet perfume. "Good, Ellie. How about you? How's the family?"

Ellie smiled. "You know Dad. Now that he's retired, he's built a small village of bird houses. I think he's given one to everyone we know."

Patton grinned. Angus Shaunessey had worked in the medical examiner's office for over thirty years. He was a quiet, introspective man. One Patton respected. But Angus wasn't one to sit still, so it was almost impossible to imagine him retired. "Give him my best, please."

"I will." Ellie had light green eyes, alabaster skin and blond hair. She was waiflike, fragile, the sort of woman a man wanted to protect. He used to. Now he hoped she'd find someone who'd do the job right.

"You look gorgeous, Ellie," his mother gushed. "I hear Mrs. Matthews retired? You're the head city librarian now?"

Ellie nodded, her cheeks flushing.

Patton listened halfheartedly, his attention zeroing in on the happy couple. His brother only had eyes for Bianca. She was equally smitten, holding Zach's hand yet blushing furiously and leaning away when Zach tried to kiss her on the lips. Was she teasing Zach? Or was she really uncomfortable with a public display of affection?

If Bianca was that…old-fashioned, it was refreshing. It had been a long time since he'd met someone that innocent. Especially in his line of work. If anything, it was suspicious. His focus sharpened, noting the flush of Bianca's skin, the way she shifted from foot to foot—her discomfort was real. It had to be. Or she was a master of deception. He sighed, his frustration mounting. This wasn't a crime scene and Bianca wasn't a criminal. He might not be happy about this party or this engagement, but he didn't have any reason to be suspicious of Bianca. Not yet…

It didn't change the fact that they were rushing things.

He nodded at familiar faces, smiling now and then. Almost everyone in Greyson, Texas, was here. Half the force was here—there better not be any emergencies tonight. His gaze wandered. He nodded at his cousin, Lucy, and smiled at the sight of his cousins, Jared and Dean, checking out women. They weren't being very subtle about it.

Spence stood apart, talking to a woman. He was smiling, talking animatedly. The woman's hand came up, tucking her hair behind her ear. Patton froze. The green dress tied at the back of her neck, leaving the fabric to sway enticingly between her bare shoulder blades.

Cady *was* here. She was here, almost within arm's reach, and she was talking to his brother. A brother who looked a little too charmed by Cady. A surge of possession rose up, urging him to grab one of Cady's soft hands and take her away somewhere—just the two of them. He wanted to touch her. To press her against the wall and kiss her until she was wobbling in her heels and clinging to him for support. He wanted to hear her say his name, broken and desperate and—

"Don't you think, Patton?" his brother was talking to him. "Patton?"

He tore his gaze from Cady's back. "What?"

Zach cocked an eyebrow and leaned forward to whisper, "Turn off the work mode, bro, let off some steam. And, looking at how tense you are, I'm thinking it's time you got seriously laid." He shrugged, leaning back. "Plenty of options tonight. So lighten up, have fun. You're at a party."

Patton smiled, all too tempted to tell his little brother how right he was. He could think of nothing better than letting off some steam with Cady. "Excuse me." He held up his empty glass as explanation and made his way to the bar.

"What'll it be?" the bartender asked.

"A beer." He kept Cady in his sights. "And a Whiskey Special, with three olives."

CADY DRIED HER hands on the towel, staring at her reflection in the mirror. She was not going to hide in the bathroom or drive home, even if she was tempted. It didn't matter that Patton was here. Just because he'd been the most erotic experience of her life—one she could not get out of her head—didn't mean she needed to let his presence chase her away. She was going to control her libido and be here for Bianca. For crying out loud, she

wasn't some oversexed teenager. She grinned at her reflection. Well, she wasn't a teenager. She straightened
her shoulders, pulled her neckline into place and headed
out to find Bianca.

She took her time navigating the curving stairway
that hugged the side of the ballroom. Her heels were
new, narrow, but too gorgeous to pass up. Still, she had
no desire to take a tumble down the stairs into the ballroom below. It was a very good thing she was holding
onto the carved banister when she saw who was waiting for her at the bottom of the stairs.

His pale eyes locked on her so intently it was almost intimidating. Her hand gripped the banister as
she wobbled slightly on her heels. Her hesitation caused
his attention to wander. From the top of her head to the
column of her neck, his gaze skimmed over every inch
of exposed skin. She felt naked, felt the heat of his gaze
so intensely he might as well be touching her. And it
felt hot. Her skin warmed beneath his inspection, her
nipples pebbling against the silky fabric of her dress as
his gaze grazed the deep V of her dress. He swallowed,
taking in the evidence of her arousal, before continuing his visual exploration—from the sway of her hips
down the length of her legs.

Finally, his eyes met hers.

She gripped the railing tighter, continuing down the
stairs while her body burned. She wanted him, now.
Even though she knew better. Once had been more than
enough. Hell, she still hadn't fully recovered. Obviously.

She drew in a slow breath, trying to douse the fire
that had her throbbing for him. She trailed her hand
along the banister for support—to keep her upright and
anchored in the present. They'd had an amazing night,

but she wasn't one for repeat performances. She wasn't one for complications. It would be easy to forget that, to wrap her arms around his neck and let him drown her in his hunger.

When she reached the bottom step, she was almost in control. She looked up at him, offering him a grin. But she had to swallow against the tightness of her throat before she managed to say, "It's rude to stare."

He held out a drink to her.

She blinked, reaching for the drink. "Thanks. Guess you're forgiven." Her fingertips brushed along the tops of his fingers. It was an accident, she'd been looking at his face—his barely restrained features. But the slight contact was so potent she pulled back, her drink almost sloshing over the rim.

His eyes narrowed, his jaw tightening as his attention wandered to her mouth.

She sipped her drink, fighting against the pull of want ready to take over. He was watching her every move, almost predatory.

"Cady!" Bianca was there then with Zach, pulling her into a hug. "You look gorgeous. Celeste said you were here—"

Cady tore her gaze from Patton's—finally able to breathe—and returned Bianca's hug. "You were too busy dancing. Like a pro, I might add."

Bianca laughed. "You remember Zach?"

Cady nodded. "The groom-to-be?" It took an effort, but she managed a smile. "Taking care of our girl this evening?"

"I'm trying." Zach nodded. "You know Bianca."

"You mean that she'd rather take care of everyone

else than let someone take care of her?" Cady nodded. "Bibi's a nurturer."

"Patton," Zach glanced back and forth between the two of them. "Showing Cady around?"

Cady risked a glance at Patton. His pale gaze was wandering the room, disinterested—almost bored. "We just ran into each other."

Lucky me. Cady sipped her drink.

"Did you see GG dancing?" Bianca laughed.

Cady shook her head. "She was dancing?"

"Zach's other brother Spence—"

"You met him earlier," Zach offered.

"—managed to get her onto the dance floor. She can move those hips." Bianca shook her head, smiling broadly.

Dancing with Spence was an added bonus. He was handsome… "Wait, *other* brother?"

"Patton." Zach pointed. "Head of the Ryan clan. The chief. The big kahuna."

Patton shot Zach a look. "She gets it."

She blew out a deep breath. Patton was Zach's brother? Meaning this whole nightmare scenario could get worse? It wasn't going to end when the wedding was over. No, she'd be running into Patton at every get-together or holiday. Not the most relaxing way to spend her downtime. She sighed. Bianca was her best friend, but she was also Cady's only family. And she'd be damned if this marriage changed that.

She tucked her hair behind her ear, her agitation increasing. She glanced at Patton again, wanting to say something witty. Big mistake. He was staring at her ear. She took another sip of her drink, resisting the urge to bite an olive off the toothpick. That would be wrong. Too much. A little cruel even. She stirred her drink.

"Having a good time?" Bianca asked, taking one of her hands and squeezing it.

"Yes, of course," she answered too quickly. "I'm amazed at how everything came together so fast."

"My mother. Once she gets her mind made up, there's no stopping her," Zach explained, slipping his arm around Bianca's waist.

"Guess it's a good thing she's in favor of you two, then," Patton murmured.

Zach laughed, nodding.

But Cady saw Bianca's slight frown, her nervous glance between brothers. It was her turn to squeeze Bianca's hand. She quirked her eyebrow, a silent question. But Bianca just smiled and shook her head.

"Hungry?" Zach asked, tugging Bianca's arm through his.

"Yes," she agreed. "Coming?"

Cady nodded, following behind them. She teetered once, but Patton's hand steadied her. She shivered, the contact of his rough hand against her bare back stirring all sorts of delicious memories up. She kept her eyes front and center, torn between brushing his hand away and turning into him.

She picked up a plate. Patton didn't.

"Not eating?" she asked.

He shook his head.

She loaded up her plate, trying to listen to Bianca but distracted by *him*. Patton hovered, steering her in the direction of their table, pulling out a chair for her, making his presence known. He sat across the table from her, against the wall. But his pale gaze always roamed the crowd, scanning, searching. What was he thinking? His face was blank, his eyes shuttered—the exact opposite of the Patton five minutes ago. There was no denying what he was thinking when he'd been looking at her. He wanted her with a ferocity that excited and overwhelmed her... Because she knew how good he was, what he could do to her with a simple touch. How the stroke of his fingers, his tongue, sent her over the edge. She pressed her legs together, throbbing.

"You'll have to excuse my big brother," Zach whispered, making her jump. "It's a cop thing—always on duty. He doesn't mean to be so...antisocial. Don't take it personally or let Patton get you worked up, Cady."

She stared at her plate, hoping it wasn't evident how worked up she was. "It takes a lot to get me worked up."

"Zach—" They were interrupted by well-wishers, who drew Bianca and Zach to their feet and animated conversation. Cady dropped the toast point she'd been fiddling with, trying not to look at Patton.

Patton was staring at her when she looked up. "A lot?"

She grinned her crooked grin and lifted her olive-laden toothpick to her mouth.

His nostrils flared and he stared up at the ceiling.

She couldn't help it—she giggled.

He stared at her then, breaking into a smile that was startling. And utterly breathtaking. He seemed to relax when she put the toothpick back in her drink.

"How's work?" he asked. "Still putting out fires?"

She shrugged. "Too many fires. Started by the boss's son. You? Rounding up the bad guys?" She leaned forward, resting her elbows on the table.

His attention settled on her arms. "Be a hell of a lot easier if they'd wear black hats."

She heard the frustration in his voice. "I know you're a cop but...what division? Or is it department?"

His eyes crinkled at the corners as he smiled. "I work narcotics."

"Drugs?" She sat back, crossing her arms over her waist. She knew the cable crime shows she watched when she couldn't sleep at night didn't compare to what the reality was like. But still. "So you must have a hell of a workout regime? Or some over-the-top hobby?" She watched him frown and explained, "To decompress? I'd imagine there's a lot to decompress from?"

He tapped his fingers on the table, nodding once.

"Play piano?" she asked.

He arched an eyebrow. "Used to."

"Used to?"

His eyes narrowed slightly before he looked back at the rest of the room.

"You're just as loquacious as I remember," she murmured.

He chuckled a little, though his eyes continued their sweep of the room. His fingers kept up their tapping.

Bianca and Zach shifted, adding chairs at their table—which pushed Cady closer to Patton. Cady chatted away, making every effort not to acknowledge the man sitting silently, driving her crazy, two feet away. She'd almost completely forgotten him when she ate her first olive. Patton stood up so quickly, he nearly knocked his chair over backward. He didn't say a thing as he headed out of the room.

Conversation stopped, all eyes on his retreating figure.

"What did you do to him?" Bianca asked.

Cady stared at her friend. "What are you talking about?"

Bianca shot her a disbelieving look and waited.

Cady shook her head. "What?" She pulled another olive from her toothpick. "I didn't do anything to Patton." Today. But…today wasn't over yet.

4

PATTON DID HIS best to avoid Cady for the rest of the evening. He'd hoped she wouldn't get to him. He'd hoped he could sit there and make small talk. But when that olive hit her lips, he knew the best thing for him to do was retreat. He'd done his part, being magnanimous with each and every family member and friend sent his way. Hell, he even danced one dance with Ellie—despite how awkward it had been. Breaking up a minor fight between two of the more intoxicated guests had offered some sort of distraction.

But he knew where *she* was every second. If she was on the dance floor, he was at the bar. If she was at the bar, he was on the veranda. Each smile or laugh, every damn time she tucked her hair behind her ear, he was sucked back into wanting her—now. And it was driving him crazy.

When the party started winding down, he found a chair in a dim corner of the porch and waited. Once Cady left, his tension would leave with her. Now that he knew he'd be seeing more of her, he'd be more prepared next time. His hands tightened on the arms of the chair. Next time.

Tonight was supposed to be about Zach and Bianca. Assess the situation, find the weaknesses in his brother's relationship, find the reason for this rush to the altar and determine how feasible ending the engagement—or postponing it—was.

The party had been great, sure, but real life was different. The day in, day out was work. He wanted to say as much to his brother, to remind Zach of their parents' marriage. To call it one-sided was being generous. Dad had been a taker, opinionated, inflexible and selfish. Not to mention his first devotion had always been to the force. Mom had been second to the job, to his hobbies, to his sons…to everything. Her life had been worry and lonely nights, slim to no praise, and four rambunctious sons to raise. Sure, Bianca wasn't marrying a cop, but that didn't mean their marriage would be easy. And going into this as near strangers couldn't help. Zach needed a wake-up call, to be reminded what marriage was. And since no one else was willing to broach the subject from a realistic point of view, Patton had no choice but to do it himself. That had been the plan anyway.

Somehow Cady had changed that. Instead of watching the interaction between Bianca and his brother, he'd been fascinated by the dip in her lower lip when she spoke. When he should have been familiarizing himself with Bianca's family and friends, he'd been hypnotized by the curve of Cady's neck and the slight angle of her chocolate-brown eyes. She got to him. And he didn't like it.

He closed his eyes and rested his head on the headrest. He didn't need this—any of it. Not Cady or Zach or this harebrained engagement. He was exhausted. Tense. Worried. Weeks like this made him wonder why he didn't look into another line of work. The latest tip had led him down a long path to nothing. Tomorrow he'd start again. A new string of shake-and-bake meth had hit the market. The car explosion on the state line had been another headache. Traces of cold tablets and a few everyday household chemicals hinted that they were facing mobile meth labs, but no one knew who or where. Their normal sources had no leads. At least, no one was admitting to it.

"You sure you don't want to stay tonight?" Bianca's voice. "There's a block of rooms reserved."

"If I leave now I'll get back before it's too late." Cady answered. "Have to go in to work for a few hours tomorrow."

His eyes opened, watching the two of them hug.

"Bibi," Cady's voice was low.

"Please don't," Bianca interrupted. "I know you're not excited about this. But I am. So, for me, because you love me, please get excited with me?"

So Cady wasn't thrilled over this engagement either? Interesting.

Cady hugged her again, pressing a kiss to her cheek. "I do love you." She laughed. "Enjoy the rest of your evening… And that energetic fiancé of yours." He heard the innuendo in Cady's voice and felt his pants tighten.

"Cady." Bianca sounded legitimately shocked. "Be careful driving. The roads are so dark and curvy."

Cady waved, then walked down the steps, her green dress fanning out on the evening wind before she disappeared from his view. He was getting what he wanted. Her—gone.

He gripped the arms of the chair, forcing himself to stay put. He would sit there until she got in her car and drove away. *Not* get up and follow her.

He sat, waiting, listening for the sound of a closing door or the roar of an engine. His eyes scanning the road for some sign of her departure. The longer he waited, the more frustrated he became. He pushed out of his chair, searching the dark as he crossed the porch. He saw her, illuminated by strands of white lights and several tiki torches, walking across the lawn toward the lake. She wasn't getting in her car. She wasn't leaving.

And he was going after her.

Every step he told himself he was headed for trouble. This attraction was combustible. Now that they were bound by more than this out-of-control physical connection, he'd be smart to turn and run the other way. But when she glanced over her shoulder, the ghost of a smile on her mouth, he gave up. He followed her, he had to. She wanted him to. And he wanted her.

She wandered toward one of the cabanas, circling a fire pit before she stopped, her gaze locking with his through the flames. He kept moving until she was within arm's reach. He froze, wishing he had some logical explanation for his behavior. He was following her around like a dog in heat. Telling her he needed her so bad it hurt probably wasn't the best way to start. Or the most reassuring thing to hear either. But it was the only explanation he had.

So he didn't say anything. His hands cupped her cheeks, tilting her head back. In the shadows cast by the fires, her eyes were fathomless, and he could see the hunger on her face…hear the rasp of her aroused breathing.

She ran a hand through his hair before taking his hand and leading him into the cabana. The building was small, one solid back wall with rolled-up bamboo sides. He watched her untie the bamboo, her fingers tripping over the knots. She'd known he was watching her, wanting her, and brought him here. Because she wanted him, too. His heart picked up, his lungs emptied and his body grew rock hard. She couldn't crave him the way he did her, but it didn't matter. He remembered the feel of her, the taste of her. And he couldn't wait to have her again.

She had two sides down when he pulled her back against his chest. She shuddered, her head falling back against his shoulder as his hands roamed across her stomach. He pinned her hips against his, his erection pressing against the soft curve of her ass. His mouth descended on her shoulder. She tasted like heaven and felt even better. When his teeth latched on to her earlobe, she melted into him, reaching up to wrap her arms around his neck.

His hands slid up her sides, his fingertips tracing the outer swell of her breasts. Her husky breath filled the cabana, a soft moan escaping as her hands twisted in his hair. Knowing she wanted him—the way he wanted her—was empowering. He caught her chin, angling her head, ready to kiss her. Her brown eyes were glazed, and her lips parted in invitation.

His mouth claimed hers. He'd never felt so desperate. So hungry. So uncontrolled. Something about her in his arms. She turned, pressing her curves against him as her mouth opened to him. His tongue thrust deep into the heat of her mouth, making her groan. He gripped the back of her head, holding her closer. She clung, hands tugging his shirt free from his pants. Soft fingers traced his waist, sharp nails scoured his back. His body responded, demanding more. He held her so tightly he worried he'd crush her. But when he tried to put space between them, she whispered, "No," before kissing him in a way that left no room for misinterpretation.

His shirt was gone. His pants unfastened. He untied her dress, choking back a moan at the feel of her breasts filling his hands. He bent, nipping and kissing each peak until they were hard and Cady was frantic. He liked her like this, wild and out of her mind for him. He laid her on one of the chaise longues, holding her head as he kissed her.

His hand slid beneath her skirts, cupping her buttock.

"You're so damn soft," he bit out as his fingers trailed the edge of her panties.

She didn't say anything, but her gaze never left his face.

He tugged her panties down, unable to stop his groan when her legs opened for him. Seeing her sprawled breathless and waiting on that chaise was the hottest thing he'd ever seen. He knelt between her legs, pulling her hips to the edge of the chaise. She stretched her arms up, holding on to the back of the chaise.

He was lost in the silk of her skin beneath his hands. Her toned legs wrapped around his hips, the heat of her core inviting him closer. The noise he made as he slid into her tight warmth was part curse, part roar—but he couldn't stop it. All he knew was he was where he needed to be.

CADY'S LUNGS EMPTIED. *Patton... Oh, Patton.* Her body was his when she was with him. Something about the way he looked at her. Touched her. Filled her. She couldn't get enough.

He moved leisurely, almost leaving her before sliding deep. Her body adjusted to his size, submitting to the power and seduction of his rhythm. Each stroke hit deep, teasing that spot inside and drowning her to pure sensation—over and over. He was relentless, pushing her to her limits. She tightened her legs around him, wanting more. "Patton," she murmured, his name a broken moan.

"I've got you," he ground out, thrusting home. Once. Again. The light dusting of hair on his chest brushed against her inflamed skin, and it was too much. She clung to the chaise lounge, her body rocking with him.

His tongue flicked her nipple, teasing, light, then sucking it deep in his mouth. She groaned, broken and raw. She wasn't usually a vocal lover, but with Patton...

She reveled in each touch, each sound. The feel of his stubble on her breasts and stomach. The deep groan when she let go of the chaise longue and gripped his hips. The decadent slide of his flesh against hers. She felt the rapid tensing of her body and welcomed the promise of release. He arched back, his hands caressing her throat and stomach, before they pinned her hips in place. She writhed, wanting to press against him, but he held her still—drawing out her pleasure, heightening every sensation. One hand cupped her cheek while the other slid between her legs. His finger was featherlight against the tight bud between her legs. Her body shook, his fingers working her over. She stared up at him, willing to beg for more. She hadn't been prepared for his raw hunger, his locked jaw and flared nostrils. But seeing him like that made her body convulse, clenching tightly around him, racked with wave after wave of her release.

His groan was ragged, his fingers biting into her hips as his climax tore through him. She watched, alarmingly aroused by the pure carnal power of it.

He rested his head on her chest, his ragged breathing soothing and tormenting her still-tingling skin.

She lay there… The realization of what she'd done hitting her. She'd broken her rule. A one-night stand meant one night. No complications, no expectations, no…entanglements. Why did she break her rule with *this* guy? When they would be thrown together again and again.

Panic gripped her.

She had to leave. But Patton lay atop her. And he smelled like heaven—felt like heaven. She was distracted by the brush of his fingers against her side, the scratch of his whiskers against her breast. Her breath faltered. She'd just had one hell of an orgasm, and she still wanted more. No, she still wanted Patton. This was bad. She didn't want things to get complicated… Well, any more complicated.

She drew in a deep breath.

It's no big deal. She closed her eyes, allowing herself to touch him. He was all muscle. Rigid and delicious. Her hands rested lightly on Patton's chest, her fingers settling on the ridge of his scars. She kept her touch light, tracing the uneven skin, stroking around the muscular shoulder to his back. There were more scars. Two, circular and uneven.

"Exit wounds," he murmured.

"You were shot?"

"It happens."

She giggled. "It happens?"

He propped himself on one arm and looked down at her, his crooked grin a little too gorgeous for a woman already contemplating round two.

She shook her head.

His gaze explored her face in the dim light spilling into the cabana. "That was… Damn. Did I hurt you?"

Her chest felt heavy. "No." He hadn't hurt her. He'd made her feel alive. Desired. Cherished. And when his attention wandered to her breast, she knew she'd feel all those things again if she didn't stop this madness. A distraction was in order and fast. She asked the first thing that came to mind. "How…how did it happen? The scars, I mean?"

Everything about him changed. Gone was the passionate man who'd completely rocked her world. His face was expressionless, devoid of any emotion. He stood suddenly, pulling his pants up in the process. She hadn't realized how cool it was until he'd left her. She shivered—from the chill in the air and from Patton.

Why his sudden withdrawal bothered her, she didn't know. But it did. Obviously mentioning the scars was a bad move. Maybe it was too painful to talk about? She stared up at him, taking in the hostility he radiated. What had happened to him… She shook her head. None of her business. This—they—was about sex. Pure and simple. She didn't want anything more. If he didn't want to share life experiences with her, fine. It didn't make sense for her to get upset about it. It didn't make sense to feel…angry. But she did. She sat up, smoothing her skirt over her legs and tying her halter behind her neck.

"Need help?" he asked, tucking his shirt into his pants.

"Nope." She hadn't meant to snap.

His eyebrows rose, but he didn't say anything.

She stiffened at the sound of laughter in the distance. It wasn't as if they were alone. There were guests at the inn. And the two of them were practically on display since he'd kissed her before she'd untied the last shade. She wasn't into exhibitionism and had no desire to be discovered by someone. Especially one of the party guests… Or, God forbid, family. She'd been so caught up in Patton she'd all but forgotten about Bianca and Zach's engagement party. What the hell was wrong with her? The wedding must be getting to her more than she knew.

She stood, shaking out her skirt and running her fingers through her hair. She should have spent less time fantasizing about Patton, his incredible body, and all the things he could do to her and more time getting to know the charming Zach Ryan. She didn't know why, but she didn't trust him.

She realized Patton was watching her, eyes narrowed.

"What?"

"I'm not sure," he answered. "You're the one sighing and hostile."

"Hostile?" She shook her head. "Me? Can't imagine why." He was the one who'd broken the mood by going all tall, dark and *silent* on her.

"Thing's a little small to cuddle on." Patton looked at the chaise longue, his sarcasm giving her temper the kick it needed.

"I wouldn't dream of cuddling with you." She smiled sweetly.

He crossed his arms over his chest. "What's got you fired up?"

"Fired up?" She slid on her heels. "Lots. One, I broke my don't-jump-into-bed-with-old-one-night-stands rule. The sex is nice, but what's the point? And two, my best friend is engaged to some guy she barely knows. One thing isn't that big a deal. The other is huge."

"Bianca and Zach?"

She nodded. "I can tell you're not into emoting and caring for people, and I get it. But the few people I do keep in my life matter. Bianca is number one. She's making a mistake—"

"I agree."

She glanced at him, trying not to get caught up in the fact that his shirt wasn't buttoned up and a good portion of his chest was on display—teasing her. She swallowed. "About my assessment of your lack of emotions or the engagement?" She knew she was being catty but couldn't seem to stop. It would be easier if he didn't get to her the way he did.

His crooked grin was back. "The engagement."

She paused. "Really?"

"They don't know each other." Patton nodded. "They have no business making a life-altering decision that will end up in catastrophe. And dragging their friends and family along for the ride."

"Couldn't have said it better myself," she agreed.

He relaxed, his gaze sliding over her in that very dangerous—very promising—way. "I don't agree about the sex."

It was like someone had doused her in cold water, but she couldn't think of a suitably scathing comeback.

"I might not have the experience you do, but *nice* doesn't apply to anything about us." He stepped closer, dragging one finger across the front of her dress—across her nipple.

She opened her mouth to argue... But he kissed her. So long and deep and thoroughly that she had to hold on to him to stay on her feet. Even then, he seemed content to keep kissing her. His hands wandered, igniting her still-shaken nerves, until she knew she was caving. When he lifted his head and his pale eyes locked with hers, her panic kicked into overdrive. She didn't like the way she reacted to this man. It scared her, how out of control he made her feel.

"This won't happen again, Patton. There is no *us* and there never will be. Nice or not, *this* is over." She spoke clearly, breaking his hold and hurrying from the cabana before she gave up and threw him on the chaise longue for another go-round. She didn't run, exactly. That would suggest she had something to run from. But she didn't look back. She kept her eyes straight in front of her until she was in her car, focusing all of her attention on the curvy roads that put much-needed space between her and Patton Ryan.

5

PATTON STARED AT the girl lying in the hospital bed. He was running on fumes. He'd spent the last two hours trying to get her to talk, give him something—anything. But his patience was wearing thin. He knew Jenny Olsen from previous experience. She was tough as hell—she had to be. But this wasn't the time to pull that defensive crap. This was different. Jenny could be pinned to some serious charges, and this time, she wouldn't be the only one who suffered. She had a little boy now. A little boy she'd lose custody of if she was linked to today's incident. Child Protective Services took the manufacture of methamphetamines seriously.

He repeated, "I'm here to help."

She rolled her eyes. "I told you. I saw smoke. I ran to the house. Before I got to the porch, the place exploded."

He nodded. He wanted to believe her. But, with her record, convincing other people wouldn't be so easy. "You think CPS is going to buy that, Jenny?"

She shot him a hard look. "You're going to use my kid, mister?" Her lips curled. "Some freakin' hero."

"No hero here." His gaze settled on the burns along

her arm. "I'm saying what you're thinking. If you saw something, it might make a difference." There had been plenty of evidence of pharms on-site—and manufacturing equipment. For her sake, her baby's sake, he hoped she'd see reason and give up whatever she knew.

She stared at him. "You know where I live, mister?" She shook her head. "You don't know shit."

He'd read her file, but he knew that was not what she meant. He'd never understand her life; he didn't want to. As dysfunctional as his family was, he'd had one. A tell-you-when-you're-full-of-shit, praise-you-when-you-earn-it, pick-you-up-when-you're-knocked-down, invade-your-personal-space-and-your-personal-business kind of family.

Russ was the only exception. None of them had known what he was involved with—until it was too late. Even then, he and Spence had done what they could to cover up their brother's illegal activities. Patton knew that was one of the reasons he kept going every day, to prevent what happened to Russ from happening to other people. People like Jenny.

He glanced at her, at how young she was. "I don't think you had anything to do with this, Jenny. But what I think and what the evidence points to—" He let the words hang in the air. She could fill in the blank how she wanted.

"I don't do drugs. I don't make drugs. And I sure as hell don't sell drugs." She bit out.

"What about your neighbors?"

She pressed her lips together, staring at the wall. "I didn't know them." She glanced at him, revealing the first break in her hard-as-nails exterior. "I didn't want to know them." He'd seen that look before. She was scared. Too scared to see reason.

He glanced at the clock. He was supposed to meet Zach for dinner in fifteen minutes. The doctor said she wouldn't be released tonight—her eye was a serious concern. He could only hope a night in the hospital would give her the time to consider her options.

"Are we done here?" she asked, her irritation waning.

"Ultimately, that's up to you." He stared at her, knowing she had a big choice to make. But she needed to understand that whatever happened next was *her* choice. And he didn't envy her. He wasn't stupid. She was facing a pile of scary shit either way. If he was lucky, the fear of losing her child would help her make the right choice. "I'll check on you in the morning."

He stopped by the nurse's station on the way out, leaving his card. And did the same thing at the hospital security office. He couldn't officially give Jenny extra surveillance, but he could ask the guards on duty to keep an eye on her.

By the time he'd climbed into his truck, he knew he didn't have time get home, shower and change. Instead he headed straight to the Lassiter Botanical Gardens for dinner. A dinner he planned to use to get his deluded little brother to snap out of it. Their family had been through a lot in the past few years. He didn't know how they'd weather another storm. And that's exactly what this wedding was—a huge, thundering tidal wave of a storm that could decimate everything in its path.

Not to mention Cady. If Zach married Bianca, she'd be a regular part of his life. He wouldn't survive that. Seeing her again had been disastrous. Not only was she exactly the way he remembered her—fantasized about her—but now he wanted her even more. If that was possible. She distracted and tormented him. At work, at home, in his dreams… In her arms, her body, he had found a kind of peace. And it scared the shit out of him.

Not that his fixation on Cady was the only reason he was so set against his little brother's engagement. It was Bianca, too. Bianca Garza seemed like a good girl. But what did he—or Zach for that matter—really know about her? Something wasn't right. He couldn't quite put his finger on it, but his gut told him something didn't add up. And his gut was rarely wrong.

CADY SPUN THE champagne flute, trying not to linger over the empty chair directly beside her. Even Patton's absence irritated her. Had irritated her for the seventy-two-plus hours since she'd stalked out of Bianca's engagement party wanting to punch something. She'd put in an insane workout at the gym every evening then went home to work on coding until the early morning hours. But the restlessness wouldn't leave her. Because of him. Because somehow she'd let him get to her.

When Bianca's dinner invitation had rolled into her email this morning, she hadn't stopped to read the details. She should have. If she'd known it wasn't going to be just the two of them, she never would have agreed to come. The last thing she needed was another dose of Patton Ryan.

What she did need was her best friend, a bottle of wine and a girls' night. But how could she confide in Bianca when the guy driving her crazy was her fiancé's brother?

"Why are you frowning? You look so tense." Bianca nudged her elbow. "How's work? Charles catching on yet?"

Cady sat back in her chair, sighing. "Wouldn't that be nice?" She shook her head.

"Who's Charles?" Zach asked, smiling. "Your fella?"

"Cady's boss's son," Bianca explained. "Cady's having to teach him everything and fix his mistakes."

"I don't mind helping him. We all need a little help when we start out." She took a small sip of her champagne. "What really chaps my hide is knowing *he's* my competition. The retirement of Daniel Grossman the third, head of my division and upper-level management mainstay, was announced at lunch today. He's leaving the company, and his big fancy corner office at the end of month—"

"Oh my gosh!" Bianca squealed, releasing Zach's hand for the first time since they'd sat at the lovely table in the elegant dining room of the Lassiter Botanical Gardens. "You're so going to get the job... You are."

"Maybe. But we mustn't forget dear Charles." Cady tried to keep her tone light even though she felt that hard knot of resentment settle in her stomach.

"But he hasn't been there long enough—"

"He's the boss's son," Zach cut in. Apparently he'd been listening to their conversation. "One of the unfortunate pitfalls of working in a family-owned business."

Cady saluted him with her champagne flute.

"How is that fair?" Bianca argued.

"It's not. Not in the least—it's just the way it is." Zach shook his head.

"You've been their go-to person for the last five years, Cady," Bianca argued, clearly fuming on Cady's behalf. "You have to fight for it."

It was kind of hard to miss the adoration on Zach's face as he looked at Bianca. He smiled, a proud sort of smile, and resumed his hold on her hand.

"It will be fine, Bibi," Cady nudged Bianca. "You know me. I won't give up."

She knew it the minute he entered the restaurant. It irritated her that she could be so in tune with him, that her reaction to him was instantaneous—even if she'd yet to make eye contact with him. He looked rumpled and tired, the bags under his eyes and delectable stubble along his square jaw making him hotter than ever.

"Sorry I'm late," Patton spoke, his gaze traveling around the table. He hadn't expected to see her—that was obvious. His pale eyes widened then closed briefly. When they opened again, the muscle in his jaw bulged and there was a deep crease between his inky brows.

Great. He was just as happy to see her as she was to see him. She avoided his gaze, finishing off her champagne and setting the glass on the table. She was not going to look at him. Or watch him. Or pay any attention to him—not at all.

He sat beside her, his scent filling her nostrils and drawing her in.

It was no use. It didn't matter that she was a highly successful businesswoman. In his presence, her cool and calm demeanor was nowhere to be found. If she was lucky, she could ignore the pull and ache he elicited deep inside her.

"Rough day, bro?" Zach asked. "But I guess every day is a rough day in your line of work. I have to admit, I don't regret not taking up the family business."

Cady shot a questioning look at Bianca, leaning toward her friend and away from Patton. It wasn't much, but it was a start.

"The Ryans are a long-time law enforcement family," Bianca explained. "Zach is—"

"Special," Patton's teasing tone implied it wasn't a compliment.

Cady bit back a smile, glancing at the brothers. She paused, soaking in the genuine affection on Patton's face. He looked almost human... She kind of liked it. His pale gaze found hers, but she looked away. He shifted in his chair, his knee brushing hers.

"Looks like your party is here?" All eyes turned to the gorgeous blonde Amazon smiling at them. "Are you ready to get started?" she asked.

"Yes, please join us." Bianca smiled.

Zach jumped up and pulled another chair to their table. Patton scooted his chair closer to her, his warmth all too inviting.

"Patton, Cady, this is Carolina Vincent. She's the event coordinator for the gardens." Bianca acted as though this explained everything.

Once Cady adjusted to Patton's proximity, she saw the look of excitement on Bianca's face. Apprehension settled hard and heavy in Cady's stomach. She glanced at Patton, who was frowning more sternly now.

"It's very nice to meet you." Carolina's blue eyes lingered on Patton. Cady stiffened, knowing exactly what that look meant. Carolina liked what she saw.

"Now that you're here," Zach said, "Bianca and I were hoping you'd be willing to order something different. That way we can decide what we want to serve for dinner at the reception."

"But—" Cady almost dropped her menu. "Reception?"

"As in wedding reception?" Patton clarified.

"Yes. I'm thrilled that the couple have chosen the gardens for their special day." Carolina placed a pale leather portfolio on the table. "We have a few details to review, but I feel confident that we can get everything done on time."

"On time?" Cady asked.

Carolina's smile was tight. "We had a last-minute cancellation—"

"Bianca loves it here so we took it." Zach's adoring look at her best friend was equally precious and nausea-inspiring. "We'll have the wedding and the reception here."

"When?" She forced the word out, knowing both Zach and Bianca were watching them and both she and Patton weren't exactly joyous over their news.

"Saturday, April 23," Carolina singsonged. "Spring weddings are lovely at the gardens—with so much blooming, the butterflies and birds. A perfectly romantic setting…"

Cady knew Carolina was still talking, but she didn't hear a word. Six weeks? She stared blindly around the table. Somehow her gaze got tangled up with Patton's. He cocked an eyebrow at her, sighing deeply. Cady couldn't stop her grin. He looked as thrilled as she felt.

"We know there's a lot to do and a short time to get it done, but we couldn't be happier." Zach's voice was low, the slight edge hard to miss.

"Wow," Cady murmured, trying to pull herself together. "It's just…it's such a surprise. A…good surprise." She tried to sound excited. She did try.

"But six weeks?" Patton didn't try. "When is the next opening?"

"Two years," Zach sighed. "We don't want to wait. We've found each other. We want our future together to start. Now."

Cady looked at Bianca. Then Zach. They found each other? Fine. Great. Why marriage? Why couldn't they be like normal people and shack up until they realized how ill suited they actually were for each other?

"Two years is a reasonable amount of time to be engaged," Patton's voice was gruff.

"Oh, well," Carolina glanced at Bianca then Zach. "Of course. We can—"

"I'm not waiting two years, Patton. And, honestly, it pisses me off that you're being a jerk about this. Bianca insisted on this dinner so we could ask the two of you to be best man and maid of honor." He paused, taking Bianca's hand in his. "We knew there was going to be some…reactions to how quickly things are moving, but we were counting on your support."

Bianca's sniff drew all eyes on her. Cady's heart melted. She hated seeing Bianca cry. Especially when she was the cause of it. But she didn't know how to pretend. It wasn't in her nature.

"Hey, Bibi," Cady finally spoke up. "No tears, okay. You caught us off guard… You know how I feel about marriage, so this is…" Her voice quavered. "Well, you know. I want you to be happy, you know that. And if this makes you happy, then I'll try." She said the words, ignoring her internal scream of protest. She wasn't okay with this. But what the hell could she do about it?

Bianca nodded, accepting the kiss Cady pressed to her cheek. "Thank you."

"Good, so we'll move forward with the April date," Carolina nodded. "So you have four choices for the meal…"

Once again, Cady tuned out. Right now, she needed to get a grip. While she did her best to maintain a calm exterior, her insides were in turmoil. She was frustrated—overwhelmed. If she was a crier, this would be the time to open the floodgates. But she didn't cry. Instead she'd have to find another way to process her emotional meltdown. She reached for her drink, bringing the glass to her lips before she realized it was empty. She stared into the empty glass then set it on the table. If there was ever a time she *needed* a drink, it was now. When she looked up, Patton was watching her.

The heat in his eyes washed over her, unleashing a sudden wave of longing so intense she shivered. He shifted in his seat, pressing his thigh against hers and making her throb. Sex was a great way to work out tension. Amazing sex with Patton. Hot, hard, fast sex—

"What do you think, Cady? Do you like Carolina's idea?" Bianca asked her. "I guess I should ask if the date works for you?"

Cady cleared her throat and looked at her best friend. Bianca's large hazel eyes were waiting, almost desperately, for Cady's answer. "Bibi, you know I'll make it work. Whatever you decide, I'll be there." She smiled. "As far as Carolina's plans go, she's the professional. I wouldn't know where to start with this whole…wedding thing."

"Don't worry, Cady." Carolina's tone was a little too condescending for Cady's liking. "I have a book with a checklist of all your maid-of-honor duties. And a timeline, so there's no room for error."

Cady blinked, ready to unleash a tirade on the grinning event planner. But Bianca hugged her, drawing her in and holding her tightly. "You will be my maid of honor, won't you, Cady? Please. I know you're probably freaking out, but I need you now. You've always had my back."

Cady was choking on all the nasty things she wanted to say to Carolina. The woman had no idea how ready Cady was to exploding. Instead she kissed Bianca on the cheek. "Of course I will. I'm honored. I love you, Bibi."

"I love you too, Cady." Bianca squeezed her again before letting her go.

"Well, now that that's settled, let's move on to the menu. Patton, what do you think?" Carolina purred, scooching her chair closer to Patton.

Dinner was a nightmare.

Cady poked at her salmon. She was too raw to find Carolina and her down-the-nose humor anything but grating. When she wasn't glaring at Carolina's attempts to charms Patton, she offered what she hoped were accommodating answers to any questions directed her way. She didn't care about colors, evening weddings versus afternoon weddings or if a sit-down meal was better than a buffet. Apparently GG and Mrs. Ryan did. Bianca had taken careful notes so she could take their opinions into consideration—always the peacekeeper.

"Here's the cost breakdown," Carolina said, handing a piece of paper to Bianca.

Cady saw Bibi's expression. Sticker shock. Her dear friend was one of the most frugal, cost-conscious people she'd ever known. One thing she knew, weddings were expensive.

This marriage was a very real threat to Bianca. Her

friend might be too lovesick to see it, but their lives were about to change forever. From what little she knew of Zach, he traveled a lot. Something told her—her intuition perhaps—that he'd enjoy a wide variety of amusements while on his travels, women included. Where did that leave Bianca? Home, worrying over her new husband? She had no illusions that Zach would be faithful. She knew Bibi—marriage was forever. Bibi would stay, even in an unhappy marriage.

She risked a glance at Patton. His fingers were tapping on the tabletop as he assessed the room in that restless, intimidating way of his. Tension rolled off him, feeding her own agitation. She knew exactly how he felt. And decided a distraction was in order. After a quick glance at the others happily immersed in Carolina's portfolio, she put her hand on his thigh. He stiffened, the slight flare of his nostrils turning her on. She slid her hand up, her fingers stroking along the zipper of his pants. He was hard, throbbing against her hand. She looked at him, welcoming the raging hunger in his pale gaze. Her fingers found the tab of his zipper, but his hand closed over hers—preventing things from getting completely out of hand. He shook his head, his jaw locked and his lips a thin line. She smiled, enjoying herself even if she was being outrageous. Maybe she could lure him into a corner long enough to find some sort of relief?

"Cake." The server slid a piece of lemon cake covered in whipped frosting and a glittering dusting of sugar. Patton released her hand, shook out his napkin and placed it back in his lap.

She'd just put a bite of the fabulous cake in her mouth when her phone vibrated. She pulled it from her pocket and stared at the text. Charles was asking her about re-booting a system. Again. Even after they'd had a very serious discussion about how that wasn't a good solution and was just a Band-Aid. The remedy was to find the faulty coding and repair it. But she was beginning to seriously doubt Charles's ability to read code, let alone repair or build it.

"Bad news?" Patton asked softly.

She stared at the text, laid the phone on the table then hit Lock Screen. If she responded right now, she'd probably get fired. She shrugged, shaking her head and sighing.

"All that?" he asked, laughing softly. His voice was gravel, sending a shiver of delight along her spine.

She arched an eyebrow and looked at him. "Words can't begin." He was too good-looking—dangerously good-looking.

"Charles again?" Bianca asked.

"Charles?" Patton's voice was hard as nails.

Cady looked at him, startled by the change in his demeanor. His eyes were narrowed, his fork held in a white-knuckled grip.

"Her boss's son," Bianca explained. "Cady's basically babysitting him."

Was she imagining the rapid shift of emotions on his face? From almost fury to relief? She had to be—it didn't make sense.

"How did Charles not come up on your date?" Zach asked. "You said all you did was talk shop."

"Guess I forgot." Patton shot his brother a crooked smile. His pale eyes locked with hers, making her insides molten.

"That's my brother, the gentleman," Zach teased.

I'm not really looking for a gentleman tonight.

She remembered the way he looked when she'd said that to him. The way he'd touched her face. The way she'd wanted him, ached for him... From the raging heat in his gaze, he was remembering, too.

Was everyone at the table truly oblivious to the pull between them? She hoped so. She hoped that, in time, this desire to rip his clothes off and make him beg for mercy would fade. Right now, it was what she wanted more than anything.

And the way he was looking at her wasn't helping. "I never said I was a gentleman," Patton murmured, tearing his gaze from hers.

"Guess I hoped you'd be on your best behavior, seeing as it was your first date and all," Zach quipped back.

She remembered every wonderful non-gentlemanly thing he'd done to her. Right now, she was seriously hoping tonight would lead to a repeat performance. Patton wasn't looking at her anymore. He was no longer restlessly tapping his fingers. Instead his hand was fisted on the table.

"So, you're a couple, too?" Carolina asked.

"No," Zach answered quickly.

"Zach and I thought they might hit it off," Bianca sighed. "But we were wrong."

"It wasn't a total *disaster*," Cady teased. Patton was looking at her then, she could feel it. "We had a nice meal, a short yet direct conversation. But we skipped dessert." She knew she was playing with fire. "Speaking of dessert, this cake is fabulous."

"It is. But my cousin Diandra has a bakery. You know how GG is about family working together." But Bianca didn't look very enthusiastic.

Cady's phone vibrated again. This time it was one word.

Hello?

"Excuse me," Cady sighed, taking her phone to find a nice, quiet place to deal—as calmly as possible—with the man who might hold the key to her promotion.

PATTON COULDN'T CATCH a break. Not at work. Not at home.

Even though he did his best not to react to Cady, he was aware of everything she said or did. Her throaty laugh, her quick comebacks, the gentle smile she had for Bianca. The tenderness on her face as she melted into Bianca's hug gripped at some cold place in his chest. And every time she tucked that bold strand of blond hair behind her ear, his body reacted.

She had a piece of sugar stuck to her upper lip. He had a hard enough time not staring at her mouth without the sparkling sweetness taunting him.

He had to get control. His body's ready-and-willing response to her was bad enough. He had no right to get furious over some guy texting her. She wasn't his. He had no claim on her. Even if he did, his anger wasn't okay. But in the five seconds before Charles was established as the tool coworker that drove Cady crazy, Patton wanted to track him down and beat him senseless.

He watched Cady make her way from the room, the sway of her hips causing him to take a long, slow drink of ice water. He was on fire, willing to follow her just so he could touch her... He was in serious trouble.

"I left the samples in my office," Carolina said, interrupting his thoughts. "Let me get them and we can talk about how you'd like the space arranged. You can finish up your cake. Patton, would you like anything else?" Her blue eyes waited.

"I'm good," he answered, acutely uncomfortable. "Thank you."

"I'll be back." Carolina stood, one hand resting on his shoulder for a brief moment before she left.

"Wow." Zach laughed. "Pretty sure you could get us a discount."

"Zach!" Bianca had a horrified expression on her face.

"It's the least we can do, Bianca. After he and Cady's miserable date, we should set him up with someone who's willing to show my big brother a good time." He pointed after Carolina. "I'm thinking she's got the hots for you, bro."

Patton frowned at his brother. Carolina Vincent? She wasn't the woman he wanted to have a good time with.

"Patton?" Bianca asked. "I *am* really sorry about that."

"What?" he asked, a little too gruffly.

"You and Cady. It was my idea. One I sort of forced on Zach. I have this idea that people are meant to find a partner. Maybe it's an only-child thing?" She shrugged.

"Or your family being matchmakers?" Zach interjected.

"Or that." Bianca grinned. "I know Cady can be... outspoken. But she has the biggest, most loyal heart. Zach said—"

"You were a jerk," Zach interjected.

Bianca smiled. "You two wouldn't hit it off, but I hoped—"

"You two would hook up," Zach finished.

"*You* said that," Bianca argued then turned a bright shade of red.

Zach laughed. "Patton does need to relieve some stress."

Bianca turned an even darker shade of red. "Zach, I cannot believe you said that. And besides, what about Cady?"

Patton watched the two of them with interest.

"I get the impression Cady can take care of herself," his brother answered, smoothing Bianca's hair back and looking at her with nothing short of pure adoration. His little brother had no idea how right he was.

"Zach, please," Bianca whispered, letting his brother know just how much she disapproved of his dismissive attitude. To his surprise, Zach actually looked remorseful as she continued, "I admit, I was hoping you'd fall madly in love."

Madly into bed was more like it. He grinned.

"And while I'm disappointed you didn't hit it off. It would have been nice, since we'll be spending so much time together from now on—"

He was still trying to recover from the images of Cady, naked, in the hotel bed when he realized Zach was watching him. Bianca was still chatting away, but the look on his brother's face told him he needed to be more careful. His brothers knew him, too well sometimes. If he didn't take care, they might just figure out what happened between him and Cady.

"I guess I'm just a hopeless romantic." Bianca smiled.

"Patton's not the hearts-and-flowers type." Zach patted her hand. "Don't let it get to you."

"Found it." Carolina returned with a large black leather book. "This has some lovely sample arrangements for the Grecian ruin in the garden where the ceremony will be held." She sat, smiling at Patton. "Why don't we look through it before we go see the site?"

Patton stood. "On that note, I'll let you do your thing," he said, pointing at the book. "I'll find Cady for the tour."

He couldn't care less about where the wedding *might* take place, but he needed space.

And he needed reinforcements. Cady was just as enthusiastic about this wedding as he was; she'd said as much the other night. The other night, when she was sprawled out across that chaise longue, wanting him… He swallowed. Maybe they could spend a weekend alone, just Cady, a bed and no clothes. Maybe that would cool his response to her. Then he'd be able to get on with more important things—like breaking up this wedding. And since Cady knew Bianca best, she might be the key to breaking this off.

He wandered through the gardens, from a hot and dry desert with prickly cacti and spindly trees to a lush and humid rainforest. He was about to turn back when he heard her voice and followed it. She sat on the edge of a fountain, her ankles crossed. She'd kicked her shoes off, so one foot swung back and forth, the grass brushing her bare toes.

"Yes, Charles." Her voice was cool yet patient, as if she were speaking to a child. "That's exactly right… No…you don't need to apologize for calling me. I understand that this is new to you…"

He saw her shoulders slump as she let out a long sigh.

"It is a big account," she agreed.

Her head was tilted forward, the back of her pale neck exposed. He denied the urge to run a finger along

the curve of her neck. He didn't want to scare her…
And once he started touching her, he knew it would be
impossible to stop.

Instead he walked around her, taking a seat in front
of her.

She glanced at him. And just like that, one of her
finely arched brows rose high and her posture straightened. She went from exhausted to defiant in seconds—
because of him.

"No." Her huge brown eyes never left his face. "I
understand…Yes. I should be available after nine…No,
coffee isn't necessary." She stared at the glass ceiling
overhead, her full lips pressed flat. "Fine. Coffee—
black, great…Yes. See you in the morning."

He waited as she hung up. "Needy little bastard,
isn't he?"

He'd surprised her. And the smile that lit up her face
made him breathless.

"He is," she agreed, laughing. "This promotion had
better be worth it." Her gaze wandered over his face.
"Hunt me down for a reason?"

"Hunt?" He swallowed. "That sounds…predatory."

She nodded, a rosy hue staining her cheeks. She still
had that crystal of sugar in the corner of her mouth.
What would she do if he brushed it away? With his
tongue… He cleared his throat, shifting where he sat.
"I wanted to talk to you," he admitted.

"Talk? To me?" Her smile turned hard. "That's a
first."

He frowned. "Talk. Not fight."

Her eyes narrowed. "So talk."

No point in beating around the bush. "Still have res-
ervations about this wedding?"

She stared into the fountain, her fingers barely breaking the surface of the water. "That's putting it mildly."

His relief was instantaneous. "Then we need to stop it."

That got her attention. Her gaze locked with his. "How do you propose we do that?"

He shook his head. "We're smart. We'll figure it out."

"You don't think it's…mean?"

"Mean? No." He shook his head. "Think of it like preventative medicine. You take steps to prevent something bad from happening."

She was watching him carefully, weighing his words. "And this wedding is bad."

"If it doesn't happen, then there's no messy divorce or permanent scars." He shrugged. "You and I know they're rushing into this without thinking it through."

She sat there, staring at him. He let his gaze wander over her every feature. Her huge expressive eyes, full lips, pale skin and dramatic brows that she arched as she asked, "Even if I agree and we do try to break this off—we have another problem."

"We do?" he asked, staring at the corner of her mouth and the sugar that demanded his attention.

"The one that makes us get naked and attack each other within thirty minutes of seeing each other?" Her attention wandered to the dancing seahorses at the top of the fountain, but he could see the rapid pulse in her neck.

"It's been at least thirty-seven minutes."

"And I was ready to commit a felony or misdemeanor at the table. Which was it, you tell me?"

He laughed.

She glared at him. "And now you can't stop looking at my mouth."

He paused, consumed by the need to touch her. "Because I like the way you taste," he answered.

Her mouth parted but no words came out.

He reached out, his thumb dislodging the grain of sugar before sliding across the full softness of her lower lip. He felt the heat of her breath, her slight shiver. "I can't keep my hands off you. I don't want to. But if you tell me to stop, I will." His words were low.

His hand fell to the inside of her knee, his fingers brushing along her leg and up the back of her thigh.

She jumped up. "We need to get back."

He stood slowly, adjusting his pants to alleviate his discomfort.

She stared down at his clearly defined erection. "Patton—" She breathed heavily. "Dammit."

"It's your fault." He stepped forward.

She scowled. "It's not—"

His nose nudged her temple, drawing her scent deep. "You smell so damn good."

She stared up at him. "So do you." Her hands settled on his shirt, her fingers gripping the fabric.

He pulled her against him, cupping her hips and pressing himself against her soft curves. She gasped, her head falling back as his mouth sealed across hers. His tongue stroked deep once, pushing his control to the limits. He tore his mouth from hers. "You make me crazy, wanting you."

"You're right, this is…crazy." She slipped from his hold, drawing in deep shuddering breaths before she managed. "You can't always have what you want." She shook her head. "What is it they say about anticipation heightening sensation?"

He didn't know whether he should laugh or drag her farther into the gardens. She wouldn't say no, she didn't want to. She craved him as much as he wanted her, and they both knew it.

"There you are." Bianca appeared. "You two ready?"

He was impressed with Cady's quick recovery. "Yes, Patton was kind enough to wait for me to finish talking to Charles."

"I still say Charles has the hots for you," Bianca sighed. "Is he cute? Any potential there? It might actually be a good idea, considering how much time you spend working."

Bianca's words were like a cold shower. For the second time he reminded himself he had no right to feel this way. It was natural for other men to want Cady. He glanced at her. But he didn't want to think about that—or her wanting someone else.

"He's fine, I guess. No potential," Cady argued. "He's just so…so incompetent. I swear we go over and over the same thing, and he still has the same questions."

"Exactly," Bianca said, taking Cady's hand. "If he gets it, he won't have any excuse to call and text you whenever he wants. And you always said his dad adores you, calls you the daughter he should have had. Makes sense that Charles, who has a daddy complex, would try to win you over."

Patton followed them, considering Bianca's take on things. He had never met Charles, so he didn't know how sharp this guy was. But Bianca had a point.

"Does he have any relevant experience or training?" Patton asked.

Cady glanced back at him. "He has an MBA. I think his bachelor's degree is in business. So, even if he did take a computer class or two, he really doesn't understand coding or database management or security programming."

He didn't say much as Bianca led them out of the main building of the Botanical Gardens. He was too busy grappling with jealousy—serious jealousy. And it was something he'd never experienced before. Not that he had a reason to be jealous.

He paused then. What would she say if he asked her out on a real date? Was he seriously thinking about asking her out? Now? When the only thing he needed to be thinking about was work and his brother's disaster of a wedding. No, this wasn't the time. First things first.

He followed the women outside, toward a field with a dramatic stone arch that led into a fanciful stone temple.

"What do you think?" Bianca asked. "It's like a mini Parthenon? Can't you just see it, wrapped in vines and flowers—and some pretty candles?"

Cady ran a hand along one of the carved stone pillars, her eyes sweeping along the curved ceiling of the structure. She nodded. "It's very you."

"It is, isn't it? But GG thinks a wedding should be inside. She always goes on about some friends' wedding. It was outside and it rained so there was mud all over. She's very anti-outdoor wedding."

Carolina jumped in then. "Sadly, this is the only space we have available for at least eighteen months."

Zach slid his arms around Bianca from behind. "I'll make sure there's no rain on our wedding day."

Patton glanced at Cady and noticed the calculating way she was inspecting his brother. He stiffened, ready to defend Zach. But then he relaxed. She didn't need to like his little brother. All she needed to do was help him break this up… And spend every nonworking, nonplotting second naked in his bed.

6

CHARLES HEMBRECHT THANKED Cady for the hundredth time then surprised her by asking, "I was hoping I could take you to dinner?"

She shook her head. "You don't have to—"

"But I want to," he countered then cleared his throat. "I was hoping you'd come to the annual office party with me."

"Charles." She wasn't about to get involved with the boss's son, but she sure as hell didn't want to piss anyone off. "I have a strict policy. I don't date people I work with. And…I have a date for the party already. But thank you." She didn't have a date—but she'd get one. Since Mr. Hembrecht had asked her to do a security presentation, she couldn't really skip it.

"That's a good policy." He nodded, clearly disappointed.

Her phone barked, her text sound for Bianca. "That's my ride." She let out a slow, relieved breath.

"Interesting ringtone." He grinned. "Have a nice night."

She nodded, pulling her purse off the back of the

leather office chair in the conference room. "I will. You enjoy your weekend."

She waved at him before hurrying to the elevator. On the ride down, she shed her blazer and the scarf she had knotted around her shoulders. She traded her business pumps for some strappy-heeled sandals, tucking everything into her gym bag.

Bianca sat in her red Jeep, her sparkling sunglasses winking in the evening sun. "Hey girlie, climb in."

"TGIF," Cady announced, pulling herself up and into the Jeep. "Tell me, does cake tasting come with adult beverages?"

Bianca laughed. "We have five stops. And then Zach and I will take you and Patton out for dinner."

Patton. Of course. Adult beverages would definitely be in order. She tried for enthusiasm as she said, "Great."

"I heard that." Bianca pulled away from the curb and into traffic. "What's up between you two? And don't tell me nothing, because there's definitely…*something.*"

Cady sighed. This was one time she wasn't going to fill Bianca in on all the details. And it wasn't just because Patton was Zach's brother. "Bibi, please."

Bianca looked at her. "Zach thinks there's something going on."

She forced a little laugh then swallowed, looking out the window at the buildings and shops. "What made you think he was my type? That's the part I don't get. He's—"

"He might not be your normal beefcake pick but come on, there's something about him. I'll admit, I hadn't met him. If I had, maybe I wouldn't have pushed so hard for the blind date. I don't know. Zach had this picture of him and his brothers, they were all smiling and so cute. When he told me Patton was single, I thought, why not. You can't fault me for wanting you to end up with Zach's brother." She shrugged. "So Patton's intense and brooding—but I thought you sort of liked that in a man." She glanced at Cady. "And very handsome."

"He is *not* handsome," Cady argued. Handsome wasn't enough. Patton was hot. "But feel free to add insufferable and egotistical."

Bianca laughed. "Whatever. Think you can behave? Just until the wedding is over? Please?" Bianca asked.

"I'll try," she offered.

But the sight of Patton, plaid shirt sleeves rolled up over muscular forearms and old jeans that hugged thickly carved thighs and a perfect ass, made her warm in all the right places. She didn't want to behave. She felt it the minute his eyes found her.

"You might not be into him, but he definitely wants to jump you." Bianca giggled as she slid out of the driver's seat.

Cady drew in a deep breath. Her door opened and Patton held out his hand. "Hey."

She glanced at his hand. It was a perfectly normal thing to do—lend a girl a hand. But staring at his hand made her insides quiver. She took it, ignoring the lick of heat as his fingers brushed across her wrist.

"Thank you," she murmured.

Bianca and Zach were wrapped up in an enthusiastic make-out greeting.

"How about we get those two thinking cake and not…" Cady pointed at them, giggling.

Patton's low chuckle caught her off guard. She

glanced at him, the crinkles at the corner of his eyes only adding to his masculine appeal. *As if he needs to be* more *appealing.* She nodded, heading toward the door of Angela's Cakes. She stepped forward, away from him, looking for space. But his hand rested on the small of her back, guiding her to the door and playing havoc on her nerves. What would he do if she turned into him? What would Bianca and Zach do?

A portly middle-aged woman glanced up as they entered. Her badge announced she was in fact Angela. "Come in, come in." Angela waved Bianca and Zach forward. "It's so nice to meet you. I have everything ready, so let's get started, shall we?" Angela led them to a small table. "After we spoke on the phone, I decided classic was the way to go. I have samples of our classic champagne cake with raspberry-crème filling." She pointed as she spoke, leaving Cady dazed by the variety of cake, fillings and frostings.

"Who knew?" she murmured to Patton.

"Cake is cake, right?" he agreed.

Cady popped the sample square into her mouth, the vibrant flavors of crème and fruit causing her to groan softly. "Mmm." She pointed at the plate, nodding. "Perfectly sweet and delicious."

Patton's gaze blazed into hers, capturing her undivided attention. She shivered as he brushed a dollop of frosting from her lower lip with his thumb. She could hardly breathe when he sucked the fluffy sweetness off. Cady stared, speechless, her heart thundering.

"You're sweeter," his whisper sent a jolt of arousal straight to her throbbing core.

"This is my favorite. What do you think, Cady?" Bianca waved her over.

An hour and a half later, Cady was feeling a nervous energy from too much sugar and too many of Patton's not-so-innocent touches. Holding doors open and pulling out chairs for her was one thing. Accidentally brushing against her, trailing a finger down her knee under the table or just staring at her in that I-want-you-now way of his was something else. By the time they sat down to eat dinner, she decided turnabout was fair play.

"Whiskey Special." She didn't even look up from her menu. "*Lots* of olives, please."

Once drink orders had been placed, Bianca spoke up. "Okay, thoughts?"

Patton shifted in his seat, shooting Cady a glare before asking, "Didn't your grandmother want you to go with your cousin Diandra?"

Cady grimaced. Bianca's cousin should not be baking anything. The brightly colored, artificially flavored specimens she'd offered up had barely been edible. But, she knew Patton's angle… She wasn't sure she was ready to join him.

Patton watched as she took her drink from the waiter. His eyes narrowed as she lifted the toothpick from her drink and smiled at him. Patton scowled, but didn't look away as she slowly tugged an olive off her toothpick and into her mouth.

"Angela's were my favorite," Zach offered. "To be honest, Diandra's didn't make my top five."

Bianca shook her head. "We only went to five bakeries."

"Exactly." Zach nodded, taking a swig off his long neck.

Cady nodded. She pulled an olive off the toothpick, ignoring the faint hiss of Patton's indrawn breath. If she hadn't been expecting it, she wouldn't have heard it. As it was, the thrill of power left her grinning from ear to ear.

"Why not take your grandmother to the two bakeries?" Zach offered.

Cady sat back in her chair, crossing her legs and stirring her drink with her toothpick. She knew her thigh was exposed. She knew Patton was watching her, so she didn't bother smoothing her skirt down. He couldn't touch her here, the table was too big, but he stared at the exposed length of her thigh. She felt beautiful and sexy…and in control. She liked being in control. Liked it even more if it meant he wasn't.

Cady shot Bianca a look. "She won't go if she knows what you're doing."

Bianca nodded. "It's true. Diandra is family. Period."

"Well, tonight was a giant waste of time," Zach murmured, clearly unhappy.

"I'm sorry." Bianca frowned into her wine. "I had no idea it would be *that* bad."

"For a minute, I couldn't feel my tongue." Zach stuck his tongue out for emphasis. "It would be wrong to subject our guests to that."

Bianca's laugh was forced.

Patton's foot nudged hers under the table. "Is it really that big a deal?"

Cady knew this was one of those opportunities they needed, if they were seriously going to go through with their half-ass scheme to break up the wedding. "I kind of agree with Zach here, Bibi, sorry. Diandra's cakes were *bad*. But…" She frowned into her drink before murmuring. "GG will be upset. And she has that way of letting everyone know when she's upset—not exactly what you want either." Everything she said was true. But she should be telling Bibi to do what she wanted, to stop worrying about everyone else... That's what a best friend would do.

"I want you to be happy, Zach." Bianca's smile disappeared. "But it's hard to disappoint GG. She raised me. She's taken care of me—"

Zach drew in a deep breath. "It's just cake, hon." He rubbed his thumb along her cheek. "I'm getting what I want—you. Making you happy makes me happy, so we'll choke down Diandra's cake." He shrugged. "We can use the gifts we return to pay off any civil suits that might be filed after they eat the cake."

Cady watched them, plucking another olive from her toothpick. If he wasn't trying to ruin her best friend's life by marrying her, she might actually like Zach. She chose that moment to look at Patton. He was watching them, too, eyes narrowed and intense. But when he turned her way, his intensity turned to hunger. She trailed the toothpick along her lower lip, biting the tip before putting it back in her drink.

"We'll make sure there's lots of alcohol to make up for it," Zach said, trying his best to console Bianca.

The intensity in Patton's eyes was unbearable, so she forced her attention to Zach and Bianca. While Bianca was dabbing her face with her linen napkin, Zach was looking at her. And from the way his gaze bounced between her and Patton, she knew he'd seen her little performance.

PATTON IGNORED HIS brother's questioning gaze. It was his brother's fault he was in this situation. He hadn't figured out how to shut her out, not yet... Cady had him stuck on some sort of hormone-fueled rampage. And if she kept it up with the olives, he'd end up giving his brother and Bianca an eyeful. He shifted, his arousal making his pants tight.

Her big brown eyes were staring into her Whiskey Special.

He took a deep breath and said, "You're not giving me much time to plan a bachelor party."

"I don't need one," Zach argued.

Patton snorted.

"No bachelor party?" Cady asked. "That's unhealthy."

Everyone laughed.

"Bachelor parties are about cutting loose one last time," Patton agreed. "Before you're stuck with the same ol' ball-and-chain day in, day out."

Bianca was still laughing. "Thanks, Patton."

"No offense," he mumbled. He might not want her to marry his brother, but he had no problem with Bianca. Not yet anyway. He'd wait and see what the background check turned up.

Cady was laughing. A husky, rasping sound that made the hairs on the back of his neck stand up. He crossed his legs, glancing her way.

"No bachelor party," Zach confirmed.

Bianca argued. "Please let Patton give you a proper send-off. If for no other reason than people will assume I'm the reason you don't have one."

Patton watched the exchange. Not many women would argue for a bachelor party. He had to give her props for that.

"Any parameters?" Cady asked him, her eyes sparkling as she continued. "No exotic dancers? No gambling…

That sort of thing? If you're pulling out all the stops, then I guess I need to do the same for her party."

"Wait." Zach leaned forward. "I thought a shower is supposed to be a joint thing, right? With cupcakes and finger sandwiches and…crap."

Cady laughed. "A bridal shower is. I was talking about her bachelorette party."

"When did men get sucked into bridal showers?" Patton asked. One more afternoon of enduring small talk, family and forced enthusiasm. He and Cady needed to get to work, soon. Besides, if he didn't get her alone soon, he feared the consequences. He glanced at her as he said, "Sounds like we need to have a planning session."

"We do?" she asked.

Cady tucked a strand of hair behind her ear. He wanted to stroke her hair and suck on that earlobe. "You're the maid of honor. I'm the best man," He said, hoping like hell that would sound like a good reason for the two of them to be spending time together.

She nodded, her eyes never leaving his face. She was beautiful.

He took a long swig off his beer bottle. "Good." He hoped he'd be able to focus on getting information from Cady—versus getting Cady into bed.

"It's not like you're organizing a stakeout," Zach laughed.

"You know I'm a planner," Patton bit back. "I don't do surprises."

"Cady loves them," Bianca murmured. "What was I thinking? Trying to get the two of you together?"

"I have no idea." Cady's teasing answer was too

quick. For reasons he didn't understand, her words stung.

"I had a dream," Bianca confessed, smiling at Zach. Zach rolled his eyes.

"A *dream* dream?" Cady looked impressed. "That sort of dream?"

Zach groaned. "No, no, don't say it like that. She's been fixating on the damn thing."

"You lost me," Patton interrupted. "Why is Bianca's dream a good or bad thing?"

"I know it sounds silly but...most of the women in my family are matchmakers," Bianca started. "It's their dreams that tell them who is meant for each other."

"O-okay." Patton shook his head.

Bianca laughed. "I've only had one before... I'm still learning, reading the signs. But I had one that I thought was the two of you. I'd seen your picture." Bianca glanced at him. "In my dream you were there and Cady was smiling. There was more, but I just knew... You two, as a couple." She shrugged, clearly upset. "But I must have read it wrong. I mean, obviously it's silly, right? Right."

Patton looked at Cady. But Cady was looking at Bianca with true sympathy, her features soft and feminine. Looking at her did something to him...something more than lust.

"I'm sure GG didn't know how to read her dreams in the beginning either. And just because it wasn't me and Patton doesn't mean there's not some other lucky couple out there—just waiting for you to connect them," Cady finished. "Who was the other dream about?"

"Me and Zach," Bianca said with a blush. "I know you don't really believe in it. I guess... I just don't want to get GG's hopes up. She'd be so disappointed that my dreams are just regular old dreams."

Zach pulled her close, kissing her cheek. "You could never disappoint her, hon."

Weddings and matchmakers? Really? Patton turned away from the kissing couple, his gaze wandering the dimly lit restaurant. He felt…restless. He didn't want to sit here, pretending he was gung ho for this disaster. He was a man of action. And it was time to act. He needed to get this breakup going and soon, for everyone's sake. Then everyone could get on with their lives.

"See anything shady?" Cady asked.

"Shady?" He couldn't hold back a smile.

"Questionable? Dangerous? Risky?" Cady kept going. "Someone in need of frisking?"

He looked at her then, unable to stop himself. "Yes."

Cady's eyes went round, her cheeks coloring prettily. So she hadn't been baiting him? Interesting. There was no denying her response to him. Besides her flushed cheeks, her fingers trembled ever so slightly as she reached for her drink. He liked it.

"What's next on the wedding-planning calendar?" Zach asked.

Patton didn't say a thing. Instead he watched his brother, closely. It was possible that, right now, his brother actually loved Bianca. But he'd *loved* a lot of girls. And none of them had lasted for longer than six months. Zach's commitment issues aside, he actually had a lot to offer a woman. He was handsome, came from a good family. And he had money.

His attention shifted to Bianca. What did she have to offer Zach? Unease settled in his gut again. Yes, things were busy at work, but he needed to carve out more time to investigate Bianca—to find answers. He'd start with Cady and go from there. In his line of work he knew there were always logical answers.

"Tomorrow is on for dress hunting." Cady's shoulders were stiff, hinting at her inner tension.

"We can hit the tux shop," Zach added, winking at his brother.

"And get started on the bachelor party." Patton grinned.

"How about I make everyone dinner after? We can touch base on what needs to happen next?" Cady glanced around the table before looking at him. "If everyone's free?"

Dinner. At Cady's place. He wouldn't miss it for the world. He nodded.

"That would be great," Bianca gushed, pulling a pink leather organizer from her bag and explaining the tabbed entries to Cady and his brother.

Right, he needed to get down to business. He sat, assessing the three people at the table. He was trained for this. He should have a sense of their motivations by now, a feel for who they were and what they wanted. His instincts were good, no point in doubting them.

Bianca Garza. A nice girl. Pretty, soft-spoken and self-employed. From the bits and pieces he'd collected, he knew she was raised by her grandmother, had no siblings, but a huge extended family. According to Cady, she didn't drink and rarely dated. So her sudden involvement with his brother was very out of character for her. He took a sip of his beer, watching the play of emotion on the young woman's face. She had an easy smile, clear hazel eyes, the kind of face that revealed all… But Patton knew she was hiding something.

He faced Zach. After their brother Russ died, Zach had become the golden child. Their mother showered Zach with adoration, and their father had extended a tolerance to Zach's youthful antics and recklessness that didn't apply to anyone else in the family. Zach had outrageous confidence, charm and—normally—a strong sense of intuition. How many times had he professed perpetual bachelorhood was his idea of the perfect life? Three months ago Zach had hooked up with some model while he was on a business trip overseas. Now Bianca was what he wanted forever?

When he turned to Cady, she was staring blindly into the distance. He'd never seen her like that, thoughtful, still. She was normally in constant motion, twitching and tapping and scooching around in her chair. Now she was a statue. A statue that looked almost vulnerable. A statue he couldn't figure out but was willing to spend hours trying to.

Apparently, Bianca saw Cady's change, too, and gripped her friend's hand tightly. Cady seemed to snap out of it then, her body tightening, her fingers tucking that wayward strand of hair behind her ear. When she glanced his way, there was a reticence that hadn't been there before. She nodded at him, a slight, jerky motion. But he knew what it meant. She was going to help him.

Their dinner arrived, making small talk sparse. By the time conversation picked up again, Cady was back to her sassy self. Which made her even more of a mystery. He kept waiting for something to make her less intriguing, instead of more. He was fighting a losing battle.

"Lots to be done." Cady grinned. "I could really shake things up, take some time off."

Patton laughed at Bianca's disbelieving expression. "Cady, you haven't taken a vacation since you started working there."

"I did, that time in New York—"

"You were there for a business trip. It turned into a long weekend," Bianca argued.

Cady frowned. "What about Jamaica?"

"Another long weekend," Bianca countered.

"And the cruise we went on for my promotion?" Cady asked. "It lasted four days."

"Two years ago?" Bianca sat back, crossing her arms. "Four days is really still a long weekend."

"So long weekends don't count?" Cady asked, looking at each of them.

"For a *vacation*?" Zach clarified, shaking his head. "Not really."

Bianca smiled.

"Of course, he's going to say that. He's sort of required to take your side from now on." Cady laughed then looked at Patton and arched a brow. "What do you think, Patton?"

Patton shrugged.

"You can't ask him," Zach interrupted. "It's been *more* than four years since he was on vacation. But I'm not sure Russ's death counts as a vacation."

Patton's hold on his beer bottle tightened, his jaw tightening. Someday it wouldn't bother him to hear his little brother's name. Someday, he'd think of him and not feel crushed by the weight of tangled emotions and regrets.

"Oh." Cady's voice was soft. "I'm sorry."

Patton looked at her. Her brown eyes bore into his, the genuine sympathy on her face easing some of the tightness in his chest. He nodded, taking another long drink of his beer.

"Sounds like we could both use a real vacation," Cady offered.

"See, it is a shame you two didn't hit it off." Bianca leaned into Zach. "You could have taken a trip together, somewhere way off the beaten path. A beach holiday—"

"A *naked* beach holiday. Talk about a stress reliever." Zach raised his beer. "Sounds like a damn fine idea for a honeymoon."

Patton tuned out for the rest of the conversation. He spent a few agonizing minutes thinking about the potential of a naked holiday with Cady. He suspected they'd both need a vacation to recover. He grinned.

"Earth to Patton," Zach said. "Get lost over the whole beach vacation?"

Patton cleared his throat then shook his head.

"Man of many words," Cady teased.

"Was he this chatty on your date?" Bianca asked.

"Hey—" he held his hands up "—I've never said my dating etiquette is up to snuff."

The others laughed.

"When was the last date you were on, besides your date with Cady?" Zach asked.

Patton glared at his brother. "This is relevant to wedding planning?"

"It's not," Zach agreed. "I'm just giving you shit because I'm your brother and it's what brothers do."

Patton shook his head. "Lucky me."

Cady and Bianca laughed.

By the time the meal was over, his patience was gone.

Cady enjoyed another Whiskey Special with extra

olives, tormenting him to the point of injury. He wanted her so much it hurt. When his brother was saying a rather passionate good-night to Bianca on the sidewalk, he gave in to the urge to touch Cady. All night long, he'd remembered the silk of her skin under his fingertips, the warmth of her body cradling him deep inside her, the rasp of her breath on his bare skin… And now, with her big brown eyes looking up at him, he let his fingers trail the length of her neck.

Her shiver was the only response he needed.

When she drove away, he went home to a long, cold shower and a restless night.

7

"PEACH, BIBI," Cady argued, putting the hunter green back on the rack. "Your wedding, your color."

"Fine. Let's start with these," Bianca said, tugging the dressing-room curtain closed behind her. "No arguing with the bride."

Cady sighed, eyeing the two dresses with doubt. She tried the chiffon dress first. "What do you think?" She slipped out of the dressing room and stood on a dais in front of a three-way mirror. "It's lovely, very traditional." Not in the least her style, but she suspected Bianca would love it.

"Ooh, it makes me think of big bands, moonlight dances and romance," Bianca gushed.

Cady smiled. "Well, that was easy."

Bianca stood, cocking her head. "It also looks like something you'll never wear again." She eyed the price tag. "If I'm going to make you pay for something, I'd like to think it's something you actually like. So go try on the other one, please."

Cady put her hands on her hips. "Bibi, do you like this one?"

"I do." She put her hands on her hips, too. "But I might like the other one better."

Cady sashayed into the dressing room, asking the question she'd been dying to ask. "How are you feeling about Zach's mom's dress?" she called out while she changed. Mrs. Ryan had surprised Bibi, offering her wedding dress to her future daughter-in-law. "Guess it's a little awkward."

"She doesn't have a daughter. She'd mentioned her dress before. Apparently, Patton's ex-fiancée was going to wear it. But that obviously didn't happen."

Cady froze. "Patton was engaged?" She had a hard time imagining that.

"Yes. Ellie? She was at the party." Bianca answered.

Ellie? The one Patton had danced with. Cady slid on the next dress. "The pretty blonde?" Her throat felt tight. Her thoughts bounced forward to Carolina. Blonde, tall… Like Ellie.

"Yes. She's supersweet," Bianca answered. "It's a shame it didn't work out between them."

If it had worked out, *they* would never have happened. Would that have been better? Never knowing— experiencing—Patton? She cleared her throat. "Did he break it off?" She smoothed the fabric into place.

"No," Bianca paused. "Why are you so interested?"

Because…if he'd been engaged, he was capable of real feelings. If he'd been engaged, he'd talked, laughed and enjoyed things with a woman. And if she'd broken it off, he might have had his heart broken. All information that conflicted with the way she pictured Patton. But it might help explain why he was so gun-shy about Bianca and Zach's wedding. "I'm not," she called out, pushing the curtain back. "Just making small talk." She stepped up onto the dais.

"That's the dress." Bianca walked around her. "It's perfect. So...you."

Cady looked at her reflection in the mirror. No flounces or extra fabric. Clean lines and just the right hint of sparkle. It hugged her curves while remaining elegant. She loved it. "Are you sure?"

Bianca nodded. "Yep. Perfect."

Cady stared at her reflection. She looked great. And about as opposite from Ellie as possible. *Where did that come from?*

"We have the dress steamed and ready to try on," the assistant appeared.

"Just because you have Mrs. Ryan's dress doesn't mean you have to wear it," Cady reminded her. "Where is the dress she originally picked out?" she asked the assistant.

"I have it in the back," the woman answered.

"Oh, Cady," Bianca sighed. "Let's see what the seamstress can do with Mrs. Ryan's first."

Once Bianca was back in Mrs. Ryan's dress, Cady stepped back. The dress was gorgeous, there was no denying it. But it wasn't Bianca's style—Bianca was more princess.

"You'd look great in this," Bianca said, holding out the lace dress.

Cady didn't say anything—what could she say? Yes, it was the dreamiest wedding dress she'd ever seen. And, yes, she could only imagine how magical it would be to wear it... But she wasn't the one getting married— thank God.

The assistant walked around the dress. "Let me get our seamstress. I'm sure she'll have some lovely ideas."

Cady sighed. "Bibi—"

"I want to make Zach's mom happy."

"And Zach wants you to be happy." She paused. Wait, she was supposed to be trying to stop this wedding, not supporting it. What would cause the most friction? Buying a new dress she couldn't afford? Or seriously altering her new mother-to-be's wedding dress? She ignored the knot in her stomach.

"It's really that bad?" Bianca asked.

She stood, circling her friend. "Let's see what the seamstress says." She snapped a few pictures on her phone. "In case you want to look at it later."

The seamstress had some great ideas. But the price for the alterations was almost as much as a new dress.

Cady insisted she try on the other dress, for comparison's sake. When Bianca emerged from the dressing room, Cady bit her lip. This is what Bibi should wear, from the glittering tiara and veil to the lit-up-from-the-inside blissful smile. A whirlwind of emotions hit hard, leaving Cady speechless. Of all the thoughts and feelings spinning in her head, she held on to doubt. Bianca deserved the real deal, not a barely reformed playboy who would destroy her heart again.

"It's a beautiful dress," the assistant prompted. "And it fits perfectly, so no alterations are needed."

"It is," Bianca agreed. "But I can't really afford it."

"We have a payment plan," the assistant offered.

"The wedding is in five weeks," Bianca argued.

"Oh." The assistant frowned. "I need to check with the seamstress to see if she can get the alterations on the other one done in that amount of time." She hurried into the back.

Cady snapped a few pictures of Bianca, the difference between the two obvious. But she kept quiet as she helped Bianca change out of the dress, unable to stop herself from checking the price. Cady frowned. As far as wedding dresses went, the dress was a steal. And yet, Bianca couldn't afford it?

Which made Cady worry. If she and Patton didn't get to work soon, Bianca would be spending *more* money she didn't have to spend. She needed to figure out who was paying for what so that, when this whole mess was over, Bianca wouldn't be hurting financially as well as emotionally.

While they were ordering her maid-of-honor dress, the assistant assured them that the alterations could be done in time. As long as the seamstress started no later than Tuesday. Bianca shot Cady a look. It made Cady's stomach hurt to keep her mouth shut, but she managed it.

"One thing down, ninety-nine to go." Bianca laughed as they climbed into her Jeep. "Thanks for having us over for dinner tonight."

"You know me, a multitasker. But this is a working dinner, Bibi. I want us to go over Carolina's list so I know who's doing what, when things are due and what I can do." Because she and Patton would need every piece of information to stop this wedding in its tracks.

PATTON DIDN'T KNOW what he'd expected from Cady's apartment, but this wasn't it. It was white, sleek and modern. He'd always thought a home reflected the people that lived there. But Cady wasn't stark or impersonal. She was warm and expressive, a spectrum of color and emotions. Cady was passion.

He glanced into the kitchen, watching Cady chop vegetables. She was in cutoff shorts and a gauzy top, bare feet flitting around the kitchen. He smiled.

Zach sat at the bar with Bianca, talking about work and travel and honeymoon destinations.

Patton sighed. Trailing his fingers down the keys of the shiny black upright piano that rested against the far wall of the open kitchen-living-room combo they were in.

"Feel free to entertain us," Zach said.

"There's music in the drawer." Cady pointed to the black desk that sat against the window, overlooking the city of Lassiter below. Less than an hour north of Dallas, Lassiter was growing by leaps and bounds each year as more families sought to escape the big city. "Help yourself."

Patton almost turned her down. But then, he opened the drawer and flipped through the sheet music. Anything that might give him an insight about Cady. "You play?" he asked, pulling out several music books. Film scores. Beatles songs. Pink Floyd. Bach, Beethoven and Chopin.

"I do," Cady answered.

"She plays piano, guitar and violin," Bianca answered.

"Viola, not violin," Cady corrected. "I like the deeper strings."

Patton closed the drawer and looked at her, cocking an eyebrow. He could imagine her caught up in the music, eyes closed, intent.

Cady arched an eyebrow in return. "You do play piano, right?"

He grinned. "Just piano… And it's been a while."

"Mom tried to get all of us to play something. She wanted us to be the next Partridge family or something." Zach shrugged.

"Are your folks musical?" Cady asked.

"No," Zach admitted then laughed.

"I was piano." Patton smiled at Cady. "Spence plays guitar—"

"Chicks dig guitar more than piano," Zach interjected.

"Russ played both. But somehow Zach got out of it." Patton ignored his brother.

"Maybe all the years of listening to you guys changed Mom's mind?" Zach teased.

"Maybe." Patton leaned against the bar.

"I have an idea," Cady said suddenly.

She walked around the counter, grabbing his hand and tugging him to the piano bench. He didn't resist her. And when she sat on the bench, squishing close beside him, he didn't mind. She smelled fantastic, sweet and clean and delicious—he could get drunk on the smell of her.

"Chopsticks?" she asked.

He drew in an unsteady breath and grinned. "I might actually remember how to play that one."

She smiled. By the time they'd played the song through, they were both smiling. But she kept going, making him play faster and faster until he threw up his hands in defeat.

"You win." He laughed, appreciating the flush of color on her cheeks.

"Which was my plan all along," she admitted, her gaze meeting his.

He reached up, tucking the strand of blond hair behind her ear without thought. Her skin was silk.

She blinked then jumped up and hurried back into the kitchen. "Now that you're all warmed up, why don't you play something?"

He couldn't look at Zach or Bianca. He knew they'd seen his moment of familiarity—and what it might mean. "Maybe after he leaves. He tends to heckle," Patton said and then offered, "Can I help in the kitchen?"

Cady smiled, but avoided his gaze. "No, thank you."

Patton ignored the inquisitive expression on his brother's face. Instead he poked around the living room and wandered, wishing there was more than five large black-and-white framed prints and a few glass bowls full of shells decorating the apartment. Either she wasn't here very often or she'd just moved in. But Zach's words reminded him he was there for reasons other than learning about Cady.

"We're using flowers from the Botanical Gardens, Creative Cakes for the cakes," Zach sighed. "You've found your maid-of-honor dress."

"In peach," Cady added.

"Thanks, Cady." Zach grabbed Cady's hand. "I really appreciate your willingness to give Bianca what she wants."

Patton saw Cady's smile dim, the way she glanced at him before she smiled. "What are best friends for?"

He knew Cady was looking to him for cues, so he took a deep breath and jumped in. "Bianca's grandmother changed her stance on an outdoor wedding?"

"No, she hasn't." Bianca's expression said it all.

"She has the right to her own opinion." Zach kissed her cheek as he took the bowl of salad and carried it to the table.

"Not to be the voice of doom here, but how is that going to go over?" Patton asked. Zach scowled at him while Bianca blinked back tears. "Sore subject?" Patton asked, taking the large bowl of stir-fry from Cady. "I'll get that."

"O-okay." Cady was frowning, watching Bianca's attempt to pull herself together.

"Bianca wants the gardens." Zach frowned. "The ruin is the only choice. It's booked."

An awkward silence fell. Patton glanced at Cady. Cady was looking at Zach. Zach was watching Bianca. And Bianca was staring at her plate.

"What about the wedding dress?" Patton asked, watching Bianca.

She didn't look like a blushing bride when she announced, "I'm wearing your mom's dress."

"Are you kidding me?" Zach sat his fork on his plate. Bianca looked at him. "No."

"Bianca," he sighed, sitting back in his chair. "Why?" Patton saw Bianca's quick glance at Cady.

"I like it. I like the idea of carrying on a family tradition," Bianca explained.

Zach just stared at her. "I'm in favor of starting some new traditions. Let's start one right now—making each other happy. I love our families, but this wedding is about us."

"I know…" Bianca smiled at Zach. "I know. Maybe we should take a break from all this wedding talk? Cady, isn't your office party coming up?"

"Next weekend. I'm giving a presentation this year."

Cady glanced at the couple then Patton. "But if there's important wedding business, then I can get someone to cover."

"I thought a promotion was on the line," Zach joined in.

Cady shook her head. "It's not going to happen. With all the extra hours and training Charles is getting, I'm pretty sure he's being groomed for the position. And, honestly, I'm not sure I want it."

"All right. Who are you and what have you done with Cady?" Bianca deadpanned.

Cady grinned. "I'm serious. If my job continues to be an even split between Charles damage control and my actual job, it's too much extra work and stress. Even if they offered it to me, I'd want assurances about my responsibilities—what and whom." She shook her head. "I'm not sure a nice office and piles of money is worth it."

Bianca shook her head. "It's that bad?"

"Charles is actually pretty sweet." Cady shrugged. "However, he is absolutely clueless about the job. For every hour I spend training him, it takes me two to undo his mistakes. It's almost like he's become my full-time job. On top of my regular accounts. And the big Japanese firm we want to take on." She wrinkled her nose. "I don't know anymore."

"It's because he likes you," Bianca interjected.

"Bibi, contrary to what you believe, not every man *likes* me. Though I'm flattered that you think so." Cady laughed.

Bianca shook her head. "You said he asked you out—"

"I declined," Cady cut her off. "It's fine."

"Why not take a date to the office party? Introduce him as your boyfriend so it's clear you're unavailable—just in case Charles didn't get the message," Bianca suggested. "And it shows you're settling down, you know, ready for more responsibility."

"How does taking a *date* say that?" Zach asked.

"Cady always goes solo. Always." Bianca offered, "So it would be a statement. Surely you have someone you could take? From what you've said, they're not exactly fun parties, so take a date that will be." Bianca nudged Cady, smiling. "Ooh, there's that muscle-y guy at the gym that likes you."

Patton saw red. Was this jealousy all but choking him? It was so fast, so overwhelming, he couldn't say or do a thing.

Cady took a sip of her white wine. "Possibly."

Patton spent the next twenty minutes trying to figure out why he was reacting the way he was. While the others were chatting about movies and having a good time, he was grappling with a serious case of misplaced possessiveness He had no right to feel angry or threatened by some guy she might or might not take to her office party.

When things turned back to wedding talk, he perked up. This was why they were here. Not so he could obsess over Cady's personal life—that was dangerous territory. It sounded as if they had a few opportunities to mess things up. Apparently the wedding dress and cake were still sore spots, but he wasn't sure how that was useful. There was lots of potential with the upcoming bridal shower and the bachelor and bachelorette party. Tonight would be a good time to drill Cady for information—he just needed to stay focused.

By the time Zach and Bianca were saying their good-byes, his anger had cooled a little. And yet, as soon as they were alone, his thoughts returned to Cady and Charles.

Cady closed the door, looking at him. "Okay, detective, what dark deeds are swirling in that brain of yours? You got awful quiet there at the end."

"I'll go with you," he offered.

Cady frowned. "With me?"

"The office party."

Her brown eyes went round. "No, Patton… Why would you want to do that?"

She was waiting for his answer. Which frustrated him further. He didn't know why. He started rinsing the dishes and loading the dishwasher. He should be glad she'd brushed him off. He didn't need to be spending his energy on this. Cady was more than capable of taking care of herself. But he wanted to go.

"Are you…*mad*?" Cady asked.

He glanced at her. Standing barefoot, leaning against the counter with her gauzy shirt hanging off one shoulder. Her red bra strap caught his attention. How had this sexy woman gotten in his head? How had he let it happen? And why? "No," he muttered.

She was trying not to smile. "You're sure—"

"Yes." He turned off the water and turned to face her. "I think Bianca has a point. If you've never brought a date, people will assume it's serious. Might help. Might not. But it won't hurt." He paused before adding, "If you've decided the best thing for your career is to stay home instead of reminding your superiors why you deserve this position, then I'm sure you've thought it through." It was too easy to look at her, to watch the subtle nuances and ticks that revealed her thoughts. She was irritated. He'd irritated her. Good. Now they were both frustrated.

"Dammit, Patton," she growled. "I'll go if I want to go. With or without a date—it shouldn't matter. My work should speak for itself, the minutes, hours, days and months of my life I've given to them. I'm the best at what I do—especially within the company. If they can't see what an asset I am to the firm, maybe I don't *want* the promotion."

"Why don't I believe that?" he argued. He wanted to touch her. The moment she'd spit out his name, his body jolted awake—hungrily.

She scowled. "Believe what you want. You don't know me."

Her words were true, but it still stung. "Maybe not."

She continued, fuming, "This has nothing to do with Charles as a guy and everything to do with his work performance." She shrugged. "And the whole date thing? Sounds a little weak to me. But Bianca's always been more…dramatic than I am."

"Bianca might be right about Charles, even if you don't see it," he bit out. "Maybe seeing you with someone would help. Someone who won't hesitate to remind him you're off-limits is a good idea." His anger bubbled up.

She blinked, her gaze searching his face. She drew in a deep breath, the front of her shirt quivering. He had to find something to occupy himself with, or he was going to reach for her. Because every cell in his body wanted him to reach for her and pull her against him.

"Can this go in the dishwasher?" he asked, pointing at the wok in the large steel sink.

She continued to stare at him, flustered. "Leave it," she murmured.

He walked to the end of the bar, putting space between them. It wasn't enough—the air practically sparked with electricity.

"Bianca found the perfect wedding dress today," she spoke quickly, sliding her phone across the counter to him. "Here, I took pictures. The first is your mom's dress, the other is—"

"The dress she wants." He frowned. "Why would she choose my mom's when it's obvious which one she really wants?"

"That's Bibi," Cady explained. "Putting others first."

He sighed, nudging the phone back to her.

Cady nodded, studying the picture of Bianca before setting her phone aside.

He reached for the wok and started scrubbing, needing a distraction.

"How's work?" she asked, wiping off the counter.

"I'm trailing a meth manufacturer. A lab exploded and left one hell of a mess behind." He didn't know why he was telling her this.

"Seriously? Holy crap." She froze, staring up at him. "Anyone hurt?"

He dried off the wok and hung it from one of the hooks on the wall. "A young mom, with a rap sheet." He carried his beer into the living room and sat on the couch. He ran a hand through his hair and took a long swig of beer. "She'll end up implicated if I can't find some concrete leads. And her kid will probably end up in the foster system. She's covering for someone, I know it. I can feel it."

"Why would she do that?" Cady sat beside him, cradling her wineglass.

"Fear," he answered.

"Can't you protect her?" She frowned. "Where do you start? I mean, that's so…so overwhelming. How do you know where to look? Who to talk to?"

He looked at her, taking in the empathetic furrow and concern in her brown eyes. She was listening to him. Ellie would have tried to brush it aside, to pretend he didn't deal with real, messy situations. "I follow leads. For every five, I hope one turns something up."

She took a sip of her wine then set her glass on the end table. "That sounds…defeating."

He laughed. "Sometimes."

"Why do it?" she asked.

He relaxed into the leather couch. "It's what I do, Cady. Who I am." He looked at her, waiting, wondering why she was so easy to talk to all of a sudden. "It's my…responsibility." He shrugged.

She nodded. "How did Zach avoid becoming a cop?"

He snorted. "Zach's wired differently. He's more… impatient."

"I'm getting that," she agreed. "He seems more like the take-a-girl-home-for-a-night versus taking-her-home-to-the-family type."

He couldn't exactly argue, so he nodded again. "He has a pretty damn thick black book, I'll give you that. But he seems different. What about Bianca? You said she's not a drinker and she rarely dates, so why my brother?"

Cady shrugged. "I have *no* idea."

Patton laughed then. "He's not that bad."

Cady laughed, too. "I didn't mean it like that." She

sighed. "So…about this plan. Diandra…" Cady leaned forward, sitting cross-legged on the couch. "What if…" She stopped, looking uncertain. She looked adorable, all wide-eyed and flustered.

"Go on," he encouraged. "We're never going to get anywhere if we try to be careful about this. We don't have a hell of a lot of time. So pretend my brother's cheating on her or in the mafia or something—whatever you need to do to make this okay." He looked at her, waiting.

She took a deep breath, blurting out, "What if Diandra mixes up the cake orders?" She did air quotes as she spoke. "What if Bianca ends up with a baby shower cake instead of a wedding cake… It would shake things up and get people talking."

"Sounds like a good place to start," he agreed. "But we need…more. I think we need to send strippers."

"Strippers? To the wedding shower?" Cady stared at him, horrified. "But your mom will be there. And Bianca's grandmother—and her grandmother's gardening group. Don't you think—"

"One of Zach's exes is putting herself through law school stripping," he explained. "If I can get her to come, we're talking major fireworks."

"Oh." She seemed to be thinking it over. "So he's into models and strippers. Bianca really isn't Zach's type. Go for it… I guess." She shrugged, her eyes locking with his. Her hunger knocked the air from his lungs. She picked up her wineglass and drained its contents. He watched the line of her throat as she swallowed. She looked at him. "It's been over two days." Her voice was low and husky.

"Since?" He tried to breathe, determined not to lose all control.

"Since we got naked and attacked each other."

He was rock hard. "I thought you were in favor of delayed gratification," he growled back, aching.

"That's one option." She nodded. "Now I'm wondering if we shouldn't try something else first."

"Like?"

"Give in to whatever this is…" Her gaze locked with his, blazing and desperate.

His heart was hammering in his chest. "Could be potentially fatal." But he was willing and ready to take the risk.

"I thought cops liked to live on the edge." Her fingers ran up his forearm.

A flash of Russ intruded, dampening his desire. "Some, maybe."

She froze. Her brown gaze explored his features, picking up on his sudden shift in mood. Her hand stroked the hair from his forehead.

"My brother Russ was like that," he muttered, turning into her touch. "He lived every single day on the edge." He paused. "I don't. My life is routine. I get up, walk my dog, go to work, hit the gym, come home, walk the dog, nuke my dinner and go to bed…" His gaze ran along her lower lip. "And that's the way I like it. Work throws me enough shit. My life is orderly, controlled—"

"Boring?" she whispered, biting his thumb.

He hissed, watching his thumb disappear between her lips. He reached for her then, pulling her onto his lap to straddle him. His hands settled on her hip, grinding her against him. He smiled at the broken curse that spilled from her mouth. "So if you're looking for someone who lives on the edge, what are you doing with me?" he asked.

She shook her head, pressing against him. "Anything you want," she answered before bending to kiss him.

He gripped her hip with one hand and wrapped his arm around her waist with the other. "Bedroom?" he asked as he stood.

"End—" her lips latched on to his earlobe "—of the hall."

He moved forward, only stopping when she was on her back in the middle of her massive bed. Bold colors and patterns caught his eye. He glanced quickly around the room, instantly recognizing this as Cady's space. Stacks of books, textured quilts, vibrant framed photos… This was where Cady spent most of her time… With who, he didn't want to know.

"Patton." She threw her shirt at him, then her shorts.

When her lacy red bra and black panties sailed past his ear, he stared down at her—taking his time. "Damn, Cady, you're gorgeous." He shook his head, bending forward to trace her sides with his fingers. Her chest quivered, her nipples tightening as his touch barely brushed the dark rosy peaks. She arched into the caress, seeking his touch. He couldn't wait. He shrugged out of his clothes, slid her to the edge of the bed and buried himself deep inside her.

She cried out, her hands gripping his forearms. He stood, holding her hips up to meet him. It was too fast, the clenching of her body threatening his control. She opened her eyes, her lips parting as he continued to thrust into her. So deep, again and again… Again, so close to the edge. He sucked in a breath, concentrating on her pleasure first. He tilted her hips and slid so deep he was lost. She cried out then, her nails piercing the skin of his arms as her climax ripped through her. He watched, spellbound by the sight of her. He kept moving, thrusting until he had no choice. His orgasm was hard, tearing a groan from his throat while he clutched her to him. He ground into her, every muscle clenching from the power of his release.

8

SHE COULDN'T SEEM to catch her breath. Her fingers slid through his thick black hair, tugging ever so slightly. "You said something about fatal?"

Patton turned his head, breathing heavily. "Complaining?"

She smiled, then giggled. "No. Not in the least." She'd spent the last several hours tangled up in Patton. Hours of unrelenting, desperate, uninhibited and mindblowingly satisfying sex. She felt strangely exhilarated yet totally exhausted.

He studied her until the rapid rise and fall of his chest slowed.

The longer he stared at her, the more nervous she became. She'd never brought anyone home with her. Ever. She liked her privacy, liked going home alone when the party was over. She was the leaver, not the one that got left. But this was different. She had the urge to scoot closer to Patton, to slide her arm around his waist and rest her cheek on his chest. Even now, she wanted to touch him. To talk to him.

What if she never got him out of her system? She swallowed, rolling onto her back to stare at the ceiling.

"I'd like to go with you to your office party." His voice was low.

She turned her head on her pillow, surprised. "Why?"

"I want to."

She didn't know what she'd expected, but that wasn't it. Her heart thumped a little. "I can handle it," she argued, strangely pleased when he frowned at her.

"I'm not asking," he bit back.

Why did she find his assertiveness such a huge turn-on? She rolled onto her stomach, resting her cheek on her hands. "You're bossy."

"I've heard that before." His hand rested on the curve of her rear.

She closed her eyes, pleasantly exhausted. She sighed.

"Tired?" he asked.

She opened her eyes. "Are you up for another round?"

He laughed. "Give me…twenty minutes."

She glanced at the clock, grinning. "I'm timing you."

"Have any other ideas for the wedding shower?" he asked, his fingers stroking along her spine.

"For wrecking it, you mean?" She sighed.

He looked down at her. "Having second thoughts?"

"I don't want to hurt Bianca," she explained. "I mean, that's the point, right? To prevent her from getting hurt?"

"Yes. Not just Bianca, though. This wedding affects more than just the two of them."

Her gaze lingered on the bullet scars on his chest. "Why don't you ever try to protect him? Zach, I mean? You're his brother. Shouldn't you jump to his defense?"

"I love Zach." Patton's voice was low, thoughtful. "But he's had a lot of girlfriends."

"Like how many?"

Patton shook his head. "A lot… And some not so long ago."

"Did he ever bring these girls home?" Cady asked.

Patton shook his head.

"Did he ever say he loved them?"

Patton shook his head again. "I'm not saying he doesn't care about Bianca. I think he does. But marriage? No."

Cady watched Patton's face, hesitating before she asked, "Is this because of your engagement? That you're not a fan of the whole weddings and marriage thing?"

He lifted an eyebrow. "No."

She waited but he just looked at her. "O-okay." They didn't need to bond over their thoughts and opinions on marriage, they just needed to work toward the common goal. "So, the shower. It can't be too overt. I don't want this to all fall apart *and* lose my best friend in the process. And I'm pretty sure you want to piss off as few people as possible."

He nodded. "Will your parents come?" he asked.

Where did that come from? "I hope not." She shook her head. "They're not invited."

There was no denying the surprise on his face. "They're not?"

"I haven't seen my parents in a few years…" She thought about it. "They stopped in Dallas for a layover and we had dinner."

"You had dinner? A few years ago?" he asked. "I have dinner with my entire family once a week. And when I mean entire I mean anyone who can claim any distant sort of relation gets fed."

Cady believed him. "We're more the drop-me-a-post-card-when-you're-coming-to-town type." She shrugged.

His gaze searched her face, the scrutiny a little too intense for her liking.

"We're different," she added. "Not all families like to get together, Patton."

His gaze didn't waver, and he still didn't say anything.

"I had unlimited funds and a great boarding school education, but I never had parents. They were always off, having great adventures, together or with whoever they were seeing at the moment."

Patton frowned. "Why not divorce?"

"Why bother? An open marriage suited them. They live their lives the way they want to. My grandparents have lived separately for years, and they claim to be happy. It seems to be working for my parents, too. The real question is why get married? Ever?" She forced a smile, trying not to feel hollow inside.

Patton stared at her, his expression unreadable.

"Bianca was the first person to notice when I stayed out all night or had a bad day. She was—is—my family. Her family may not have had much money, but they gave generously of their time and affection." She paused. She'd never really told anyone that before, except Bianca. And she didn't know why she was telling him. She drew in a deep breath, quickly adding, "You know how that is, I guess. I went with Bianca to pick up your mother's wedding dress, which is gorgeous by the way, and saw all the pictures. It's obvious you grew up in a happy home with parents who are proud of you."

"I guess I did. Dad wasn't exactly the warm-fuzzy type—"

"Huh, go figure," she interrupted, grinning at him.

His foot poked out from under the blanket and nudged her. "But there was never a doubt that we were loved."

"It must have been hard on them." She nodded at his scars.

"It was." He stiffened, his expression shuttering before her eyes. "Not because of this." He tapped the two scars. "But because this happened when Russ was killed."

"I'm sorry, Patton. I'm so sorry." She threaded her fingers with his, not sure what to do or say.

He glanced at her hand, then his gaze met hers. She'd never seen so much grief. Listening to him, she felt his pain and sadness. "I won't lie, it was the worst damn day of my life. Russ worked narcotics with me. He was undercover, a real natural..." He shook his head. "I was in charge of the operation—a sting, nothing unusual. We had it covered, we knew what to expect—how many we were up against. But our intel was wrong and Russ was there... He shouldn't have been there." He paused. "Someone got jumpy and bullets started flying. Russ bled out on the way to the hospital. Another officer died at the scene. Everyone kept telling me how lucky I was. All I could think about was my brother...and my parents crying."

She didn't think as she dropped the sheet to hold him close. "It's not your fault. You know that, right? I mean..." She stopped. She had no idea what she was talking about. She stroked the side of his face, murmuring, "You *are* lucky."

"To be alive? I know." His hands clasped her upper arms, pulling her tight against him. "Right now, I'm feeling pretty damn lucky." His voice was a low growl. His mouth latched on to her bottom lip. "You make me feel alive, Cady."

She knew exactly how he felt. Her body reacted instantly to him. She wanted him, again—still. Which meant she wasn't cured of her Patton addiction. But was he cured? That strange nervousness made her heart thump like crazy. "So this didn't work?" she asked between kisses.

"What?"

"You're not...tired of me?" she asked.

He barked out a laugh. "Tired?" he asked, rolling her under him. He rested on his elbow and pulled the blanket back. His gaze traveled slowly from the top of her head to the tips of her toes. When he was done, he shook his head and flopped onto his back—his breathing accelerated again.

She turned onto her side, running her fingernails along his side, hip and thigh. His instant arousal impressed her. Especially considering the last few hours. But she understood. She wanted him again, too, badly. "We can't keep doing this."

"I know," he agreed. "It's a distraction. One we don't need."

How could she ache for him when he was right beside her? It was time to be done, to cut off this addiction they had for each other. "No more."

He nodded, his attention fixed on her lips. "One last time," he said, meeting her gaze.

She couldn't stand it then. "One last time," she murmured, kissing him with a desperation she'd never felt before. His arms caught her, pressing her tightly to him. She slid on top of him, groaning as her body enveloped him. His hands gripped her hips, arching into her until there was no space between them.

"You're going to kill me," he ground out.

"Die happy," she sighed, rolling her hips.

His broken "Cady" pushed her higher. His hands and mouth roved over her body. His hands tangled in her hair, pulling her down. When she moved, his tongue pushed into her mouth, mimicking the actions of their bodies.

Their lovemaking was hard and fast, both of them shouting their releases before collapsing into a heap on the bed. But Patton caught her to him, cradling her against his chest in a way that clutched at her core. The beating of his heart beneath her ear, the way he breathed deep in her hair... She was entering foreign territory here, and it scared the crap out her.

She drew in a deep breath, hoping to relax, when he asked quietly, "Work from home often?"

"Sometimes," she murmured. "No more than a couple of days a week."

"I'm guessing you spend more of your time in here," he continued.

How did he know? "Why?" she asked.

"The apartment. This is the only room that's...you." His hand stroked her back. "The rest is impersonal, neutral—like you don't want to let people see the real you." He pointed around the room. "This. Colorful, welcoming, comfortable and not nearly as together as you'd like the world to think," he finished.

She swallowed. "Um, is there a compliment in there somewhere? 'Cause I think I missed it."

"It wasn't meant as an insult. I guess I'm wondering why you let me in?" he asked, staring down at her.

"I don't know." She frowned, realization hitting her hard. "Other than Bianca, no one else has ever been in this room." She regretted the words as soon as she said them. She didn't know why it mattered, but it did.

His gaze was heavy, unwavering…piercing.

Panic set in. She didn't want to do this. She didn't want *emotions* getting in the way, dammit. But, right now, her emotions were freaking her out. Yes, he'd done things to her body, made her feel things that no one else ever had. Somehow, it was more than that. For the first time in her life, her heart was involved, and it scared the shit out of her. She'd spent her whole life guarding herself, preventing herself from feeling any misguided and sentimental crap for a man. But none of that seemed to matter now. Because even though she'd never fallen in love before, she was pretty sure falling in love with a man she had nothing in common with was a very bad idea.

Wait… Love? With Patton? No. No way in hell she was going to let that happen. She was doing just fine on her own. Hell, she liked being on her own. She ignored the sharp pain in her chest and pushed out of his arms. She didn't need him. Without a backward glance, she hurried into the bathroom. "Shower," she called out before closing the door and having a panic attack.

PATTON STOOD OVER the grill, flipping the hot dogs and hamburgers while his brother and cousins debated the same old things—whose truck was better, which football team was better, what beer was better and what his mother had made for dessert. She never told anyone, just to see what they came up with.

He'd always been the big brother to them—too big to be part of the group and too mature to want to be. Zach and Spence had always been supercompetitive. His cousins, Dean and Jared, were about the same age. They'd grown up three blocks over and, ever since they could ride bikes, the four of them had been getting into trouble. Five when Russ was around. Russ had always been good at finding trouble. When Spence and Russ joined the force, Jared and Dean joined with them. Every task, every test and every certification had been a contest. But when Spence and Russ went into narcotics, Jared and Dean had followed their father into homicide.

"Don't forget about my meatless patties," Lucy said, putting a plate beside him.

"Like you'd let that happen?" he asked, smiling at his cousin.

Lucy was Dean and Jared's little sister. She was a character—strong willed and vocal. But that was probably because she was the only girl amongst very loud, very rambunctious male cousins. Even outnumbered, she almost always got her way. She smiled broadly. "Thanks for cooking. I brought an extra in case you want to try one?"

"No, thanks. It's not a burger without meat," he argued. "Even Mikey would know that."

Mikey raised his head off his paws to look at his master, his tail thumping.

"No food," Patton said. "Not yet, Mikey."

Mikey yawned and rested his head on his paws again, looking bored.

"I bet Mikey would think they're yummy," Lucy

cooed at the dog, going to sit by the large yellow lab that was, truly, Patton's best friend.

Mikey rolled over, offering Lucy his stomach.

"He has a real eye for the ladies." Patton laughed at his dog's antics.

"Don't burn those," his mother called out as she walked by, carrying a bowl with a mountain of potato salad.

"Yes, ma'am." No point in arguing with her. He knew what he was doing. He'd been the grill master since his father's death, and he'd yet to burn a piece of meat.

"Don't you sass me," his mother shot back.

He smiled. He needed this—the normalcy and routine. He needed a few hours of no drama, no work and no distractions—

"Bianca's here," Zach called as he hurtled out the back gate and headed toward the street.

Patton looked through the gate to see Cady's little gray sports car parking along the curb. His hand tightened on the spatula, and his chest felt heavy.

"Is that Cady's car?" his mother asked. "Spence, go get her. We need to put some meat on that girl's bones." She walked over to Patton, watching Spence head toward the gate. "I think Cady might just hit it off with your brother. What do you think?"

It was a good thing his mother was staring after Spence, otherwise she'd pick up on his disposition. He'd been in decent spirits—almost chipper. But now that he was thinking about Spence and Cady, his mood took a nosedive. He speared one of the hot dogs with too much force, knocking it off the grill and onto the grass. Mikey snapped it up in a heartbeat.

"Who's Cady?" Lucy perked up.

Patton glanced at her. Great, she'd seen his little outburst. He had no doubt his cousin, the psychiatrist for Greyson Police Department, was analyzing the shit out of him. He glared at her as she hopped up and headed to the fence to join his mother. He sighed.

"What's up?" Dean asked.

"The hot chick is here," Jared informed his brother. "The one I danced with at the engagement party."

Dean snorted. "I danced with her, too."

Patton flipped a burger and took a long swig of his beer.

"Is she dating anyone?" Dean asked him.

"Why would I know?" he asked.

"You've spent a hell of a lot of time with them the last couple of weeks. If she was seeing someone, that would have come up by now," Jared jumped in.

He'd seen a lot of her—he'd seen all of her. "Not that I know of," Patton muttered, lifting some burgers from the grill and putting them on a platter. "Why don't you make yourself useful?" He offered the tray to Jared.

Jared took it, eyebrows high. "Sure, no problem."

He heard Dean's whispered "What's eating him?" but ignored it. He didn't like being moody any more than his cousins did. When the garden gate squeaked, he tried not to look up. Maybe it was only Zach and Bianca. Cady could have turned down Spence. He really hoped she had. Hopefully, she was just dropping Bianca off and was heading to her apartment.

He glanced up to find Cady shaking hands with his cousin Jared. Jared, who was making a fool of himself over Cady.

Seeing her shouldn't make him feel this way. Happy, relieved and excited. He slapped the spatula against a burger. He had no right to feel any of those things. He'd seen the panic on her face when they crossed the line from playful to…intimate. Not intimate as in sex, but intimate as in baring their scars and thoughts to each other. She didn't want to go there with him. Her confession, words that had shaken him to the core, had her practically running into her bathroom. He'd sat there, happier than he'd been in years, waiting for her to come out. But her shower had lasted forever, and he knew what she was doing. She wanted him to go. He'd tugged on his clothes and left, hoping he'd get used to the hole in his chest and the pain twisting his stomach. Whatever feelings he was having, they'd go away in time. For now he should be happy she wasn't out and about, being available.

Then again, his mom was assessing Cady, clearly sizing her up for one of the Ryan men. And Spence… Well he couldn't exactly blame his little brother for appreciating just how appealing Cady was. She was all woman, her navy sundress with big white polka dots showing off just how feminine and pretty she was. He admired her ankles, her bright red shoes and the creamy skin of her calves.

He blew out a long, slow breath and turned his attention back to the grill. He had to keep it together. His family would bombard him with questions if he let on that he was…interested in Cady. He slapped Lucy's burgers on the grill and patted the nonmeat into place with vigor.

"Patton, you okay?" his mother asked.

"Great. Jared took the burgers to the table," he spoke without looking up. "Hot dogs are ready." He handed her the pan with hot dogs.

His mother took the pan but stared at him. "What's eating you?"

He shook his head. "Nothing."

"Patton Joshua Ryan, I know when something's weighing on you—"

"I'm fine, Mom," he said, holding up both hands—and his spatula. "No need to use the middle name."

But his mother stood her ground, her brow furrowed and her mouth in a small, tight frown.

"You're in trouble," Zach said as he, Bianca, Spence and Cady approached. "Middle names are like curse words—you hear them, you better start running."

"And whose middle name did we hear most often?" Patton asked, glancing at his brother.

"Yeah, Zachary David?" Spence asked.

"Oh, really, we're going to go there, Spencer Lee?" Zach bit back.

Their mother was laughing now. "All right, all right." She shook her head. "You're too young to act so serious, Patton." She stood on tiptoe to kiss his cheek. "Don't be such a bear all the time."

He knew she meant well, but he also knew that if he wasn't serious—if he wasn't the head of the family—things would fall apart. It had nothing to do with ego and everything to do with responsibility. His father had relied on him as a man, not a boy. And his brothers had always looked up to him as a role model, not a friend.

"How are you, Patton?" Bianca hugged him.

"Good. Probably smell like barbecue," he said as he hugged her awkwardly with one arm. He shot a questioning glance at Zach. He wasn't exactly a hugger by nature—something his brother knew well. Zach just smiled.

"Looks good." Bianca stood there, looking uncomfortable. "Can I do anything?"

"Nope," he answered. "Got this down to an art."

Bianca nodded, glancing at Zach, who shrugged.

What the hell was going on?

"What would you like to drink?" Spence asked, all smiles.

"Oh, some tea would be lovely." Bianca glanced at Patton's empty beer bottle. "Your beer is empty. I'll get you a new one." And with that, she and Zach disappeared into the house.

Patton stared after Bianca, confused.

"She thinks you don't like her," Cady's voice was low and husky, rolling over him and setting his nerves on edge and his hunger on fire. He glanced at her, but she didn't look at him.

"Patton doesn't like many people," Spence teased. "But he sort of hugged her and he did say more than two words to her, so she should feel pretty good right now."

Patton ignored his brother. He'd much rather talk to Cady…and get her to look at him. "Did she say why she thought I didn't like her?" He drew in a deep breath and looked at her, really looked at her. It was hard work, not staring at those full red lips or the ear she exposed when she tucked her blond streak of hair behind it.

Cady shook her head. "She wants you to like her—since you'll be family soon." She glanced at him, her brown eyes sweeping over his face before she looked away. "What an amazing garden."

"Mom takes a lot of pride in it," Spence offered. "There's some rose tour the Horticulture Society has every fall—it's sort of a big deal—she gets kind of crazy over it. She and Bianca are two peas in a pod. Do you garden?"

Patton heard the nervousness in his brother's voice. So Spence was interested in Cady. His stomach felt cold and hollow.

"No." She laughed. "Bibi's got the green thumb. I'm good at *not* gardening."

"No gardening." Spence teased, "What sort of hobbies does a high-power executive have?"

Patton watched her closely. He'd seen her naked, touched her, tasted her, but he had no idea what she liked to do with her spare time. Had he always been such a dick? It wasn't as if he didn't want to know her— he did. But whenever they were together things got carried away. His attention wandered to her mouth… He tore his gaze from her, directing all of his attention on cleaning up his work space.

"I play music and I work out," she admitted, almost shyly. "I work out a lot." She shrugged.

Patton grinned. He did know that. The working out made sense; she didn't like to sit still.

"Hey, you must be the best friend?" Lucy held out her hand to Cady. "I'm the cousin. One of the cousins. Actually, the only girl cousin. Out of nine. Feel free to sympathize."

Cady took her hand, laughing. "I'm not sure what to say to that. Except…wow."

Lucy nodded. "Yep." She glanced at Spence then at Patton. "So you know these Ryan brothers. But there are more. My brothers—" she turned and pointed "—are over there. Dean and Jared. I know they look a lot alike, but Dean's hair is a little blonder. And Jared has a scar through his eyebrow. They're trying to act like they're not checking you out right now. But Jared is totally checking you out." She paused, glancing at Patton so quickly he almost missed it. "They're single and sweet—in case you're interested?"

Patton glared at her. Lucy's smile was huge. He realized what she was up to then and felt like a complete idiot. She was trying to figure out his feelings. And, boy, had he taken the bait.

9

CADY HAD DONE her best to avoid him, she'd had to. She'd never felt so out of control. One moment she wanted to tell him everything—to admit she was falling for him. The next, she knew she needed to keep her mouth shut and get the hell out of there. When they were done destroying this engagement, they were done, too. How could there possibly be a future for them? When Bianca and Zach were so important to their lives.

When Patton started cleaning up outside, she offered to help tidy up inside. As long as she kept some distance between them, she'd make it through the night. She was covering bowls of green beans and potato salad with plastic wrap when Bianca came in.

"What's going on with you?" Bianca asked, placing the fruit salad on the counter. "What is up between you and Patton?"

"I don't know what you're talking about." Cady looked at her as if she was crazy.

"Come on, Cady. He's been watching you since we got here." She sounded excited, almost hopeful. "There's this weird tension between you."

He'd been watching her? Every time she'd dared look his way, he seemed completely oblivious to her. Cady shrugged. What could she say?

"Nothing? Really?" Bianca prodded. "You're acting weird."

Cady shook her head, deflating a little. "If I've been a buzzkill, I'm sorry." It wasn't Bianca's fault that she was having actual feelings for a guy. A guy who had left her in the shower—no note, no phone call, no freaking email—after she'd actually *shared* with him. Had she freaked out? Had she taken way too long in the bathroom? Hell, yes, but she'd needed to calm down—to regroup. Nothing had hurt as much as emerging to find her bed and her apartment empty.

"Maybe it's just me." Bianca was talking, pulling her back to the present. "I'm being so oversensitive—"

"You've got a lot going on." Cady took Bianca's hand in hers. Bianca didn't need to be worrying over her right now. "Weddings are stressful," she added. "Speaking of stress…" This wasn't the place for this conversation, but she saw an opening and she took it. "I know things are super tight right now, and I'd like to help, if I can. It's just me. And as you've pointed out, I don't have much of a life, so it's not like I've got a ton of expenses."

"I never said you don't have a life. I said you work too hard. And you could use a vacation." Bianca frowned.

"Fine, okay, whatever," Cady teased, trying to lighten the mood. "But if you need my help, you'll let me know? Right?"

"Cady, I mean it. No secrets, I promise." Bianca shook her head. "We're different, you know that. I have to tell you everything… Too much sometimes. You know all about my money troubles, the shop's spotty business and all the family drama." She smiled. "I don't know how you keep it all bottled up. I love you. I want you to be happy. And recently, you're so distracted—which isn't like you. I'm worried about you. Whatever it is, you can tell me. I'm here for you, too."

Cady blinked, her eyes stinging unexpectedly. "Oh, God, Bibi, I don't even know where to start."

Bianca took her hand. "At the beginning? It's not work?"

Cady shook her head, her mind filled with images of Patton. Patton smiling at her. Patton's fingers sliding through her hair. Patton's lips nipping at her earlobe. She shivered. "No. Not work." Her hands gripped the edge of the countertop.

"So… It's a guy?" Bianca's voice was soft.

Cady sucked in a deep breath before facing all the questions in Bianca's hazel eyes. It was the sight of Patton, over Bianca's shoulder, that silenced her.

Patton filled the doorway, his pale eyes fixed on her. She was off-kilter enough with him standing there, looking at her as if she was dessert…and he was starving. The kitchen seemed to shrink, ratcheting up her nerves. She tore her gaze from his, absentmindedly placing an extra layer of plastic wrap on the veggie tray.

"Hey, ow," a muffled voice came from behind Patton. "Why did we stop walking?"

"You can come in, Patton." Bianca laughed.

He stepped inside. "Didn't want to interrupt," his low voice sent a chill down her spine.

She didn't look at him. She couldn't afford to get lost in those eyes…or the hold he had on her.

"At least give a girl warning, cuz. Your back is hard.

Must be all the muscles," Lucy teased, heading to the refrigerator.

Cady knew his back was all muscle, not that she'd ever volunteer that information to anyone. Or linger on the images of him...all muscles and strong, yet gentle, hands...

Lucy opened the door and pulled out a pitcher of lemonade. "Beverage duty," she explained. "For dessert. I think the *boys* are finally getting tired of darts and horseshoes and ready for more food. Bottomless pits, the lot of them."

"Right. Where are the dessert plates?" Bianca asked.

"I'll show you," Lucy offered. "Can you take this out?" Lucy held out the lemonade to Cady.

And then they were alone. She placed the covered dishes in the refrigerator, picked up the pitcher and headed to the back door. But he set the cooler he'd been holding on the ground and blocked her path.

"Excuse me," she kept her voice light and airy.

But he just stood there, forcing her to look up at him. He was staring down at her, his eyes piercing...searching. She couldn't look away. One look was all it took. The air seemed to thicken around them, pressing her toward him. The scent of him both soothed and excited her. Dammit. She didn't know whether to dump the lemonade on him or put it on the counter so she could throw herself at him.

She held the pitcher up, cocking an eyebrow at him.

He stepped back, holding the kitchen door open for her. Of course, it also required her to brush by him, sending each and every nerve ending into overdrive. His gaze stayed on her, sweeping over her face to linger on her mouth. She needed air, now. She pushed past him, sucking in deep lungfuls of cold air as she crossed the patio. "Lemonade?" she asked.

"Thank you, Cady." Mrs. Ryan smiled. "I'm so glad Spence convinced you to stay for dinner."

Spence…who was also looking at her. He had been sweet and charming and funny all night. Too bad she was into tall, dark and brooding types. She turned, glancing at the kitchen's screen door. No Patton. Which was good. Wasn't it?

"Hey, Cady," Jared called out. "You any good at darts?"

She shook her head, waving. "No. Wouldn't want to hurt anyone."

"I'm a good teacher," the other cousin, Dean, spoke up.

It was hard to ignore the creak of the kitchen door. She almost stopped herself from looking up. Almost. Lucy and Patton carried plates and cutlery toward the table. Bianca joined Zach at horseshoes.

"Oh, leave her alone," Lucy interrupted. "You're losing to Jared and you're looking for a distraction." She put the plates on the picnic table and winked at Cady.

"Gee, thanks, sis." Dean frowned at his sister.

"The only girl?" Cady asked, returning the smile of the perky curly-haired blonde in front of her.

"Yep. Don't forget Mark and Mason," she pointed. "Or the twins of terror, as I call them. I think the only reason they became firemen is because they were such pyromaniacs as kids."

Cady acknowledged the twins throwing darts and cracking jokes with Zach, Dean and Jared. There was no denying the Ryans were a good-looking bunch of men. Or that they were a close-knit family. A lump settled in her throat. "That's a lot of testosterone." She glanced at Mrs. Ryan. "I can't believe you do this every week."

"Oh, it's not always this nice. Have a seat and some lemon icebox pie." She offered Cady a plate.

Cady sat, taking a bite of the pie. "This is amazing." She took another bite, all too aware that Patton sat beside her on the bench.

Mrs. Ryan smiled. "Thank you. I normally make a casserole, lasagna or pasta salads. But I wanted to do a little more since this was Bianca's first family dinner and all," she explained. "Now that you're practically family, you're welcome to join us anytime, Cady."

Mrs. Ryan's words were exactly what she needed to snap out of it.

What was doing? *She* wasn't joining the Ryan family. So why was she still sitting here? This wasn't…*her*. She ignored the very present feeling of Patton at her shoulder—and the very real possibility that his presence was why she was still here. But why? This *wasn't* what she wanted. This wasn't part of her life, these weren't her friends or family—besides Bianca.

"Thank you for the wonderful meal," she said, standing. She needed to go to the gym, work off some frustration and clear her head. Then she needed to make sure the debugs were ready to run over the weekend for their new international client. She didn't have time for family dinners, falling in love or raging hormones. And, since none of those things were priorities, she wasn't going to make time for any of them. "It's getting late. I should go." Cady took Mrs. Ryan's hand in hers, shaking it.

"Oh, honey, we're huggers around here." Mrs. Ryan hugged her—hard. "You're welcome anytime," the woman said in her ear.

Cady felt a sudden sting in her eyes—ratcheting taut her already tightly wound emotions. But she managed to speak without sounding like a woman on the edge. "I appreciate that."

She gave Bianca an extralong hug. "I'll see you Saturday? Reception decorations?"

Bianca nodded. "But... I'd rather have some alone time if you're free for lunch tomorrow?"

Which would be a very bad idea. She'd almost spilled everything to Bianca. Once her emotional epiphany was out there, it would impossible to ignore. So Cady hedged, "I'm swamped at work. Tomorrow's the last day to make sure the big upgrade and debug goes off without a hitch this weekend. Can't lose this client— it's that big new Japanese firm, remember? *And* there's the office party."

"Knock 'em dead, Cady." Bibi hugged her, hard. "I know you'll get the promotion."

Cady made her goodbyes quickly, keeping her smile as bland as possible when she locked eyes with Patton.

"It was nice to meet you." Lucy walked with her across the yard, her words a hurried whisper. "Listen, it's none of my business, but I love my cousin. Patton's a great guy and... I've never seen him act like this over a woman. Ever."

Cady had no time to process Lucy's words before Spence opened the gate. "Ready? I figure I'll be the gentleman tonight. I wouldn't want you to get attacked in the three hundred feet that lies between here and the safety of your car."

Cady laughed, following him through the gate. "Yes."

"Should I put on my bulletproof vest?" Spence asked.

He had a nice smile. "I mean, our neighborhood is pretty shady."

Cady shook her head, the tension in her chest easing. "That's the word I'd use to describe your neighborhood, all right. Shady—from all the glorious trees and manicured lawns."

Spence laughed then.

"Cady," Patton called out, "What time am I picking you up tomorrow night?"

Cady turned back to stare at Patton. She wasn't alone. Everyone in the Ryan's backyard was staring at him—stunned into absolute silence. What was he up to?

"We don't have any wedding stuff planned, do we?" Zach finally asked, looking at Bianca for confirmation.

"No," Patton answered. "Cady and I are going to her office party." He strode toward her, all muscle and confidence. He took her breath away… But his smug little grin doused her appreciation and ignited her temper.

THE WHOLE NIGHT had been one long exercise in torture. To have her so close, within reach, but not able to touch her. Hearing his cousins talk about her, seeing Spence's spark of interest in her—he'd never felt the urge to run before. But he felt unpredictable when it came to Cady. He didn't want his attachment to her to make him do something he'd regret.

Her conversation with Bianca had left him reeling… First, Bianca was in money trouble. As a cop, he knew that was a pretty strong motive. Was Bianca jumping into this wedding for Zach's money? It was way past time to look into Bianca Garza's past. He needed answers—and soon.

Second, who was the guy that had rattled Cady? He knew who he wanted it to be.

As he reached the gate, he saw the tightening of her mouth, the slight narrowing of her eyes and couldn't help but grin.

"I'll let you two work out the details then," Spence offered. "If you think you can get her safely to her car, that is?"

Patton nodded but didn't take his gaze off Cady. Her temper was so damn sexy. It took everything he had not to crush her against him and bury his hands in her hair.

"I'll be fine," she hissed as soon as Spence was out of earshot. "But you might not be so lucky."

He laughed.

Her eyes went wide, her hands fisting at her sides. "Patton—" She paused, her attention wandering beyond him. To everyone in his family watching them. She pressed her lips together, spun on her little red heels and headed toward her car.

He jogged to catch up then fell in step with her. "About tomorrow—"

"I told you I can handle it." She glared at him, fumbling in her purse for her keys.

"And I told you I was taking you." He leaned against her driver door, blocking the handle and lock. "What time?"

"Move, please." Her words were short, snipped. "I have plans."

With those three little words his amusement dimmed. "Now?" he asked, staring down the street.

She crossed her arms over her chest and looked at him.

"Okay." He moved. As hot as she was pissed, he didn't want to lose this time with her. "What time tomorrow?"

She paused. "You're really not going to give up?"

"No."

She looked at him. "Is there something about me that screams damsel in distress?"

He shook his head, searching her face.

"Then what's the big deal?" she asked. "And what the hell was that?" She waved at his mother's house.

He knew deep down why it was a big deal...why he'd just made Cady off-limits to the rest of the Ryan men. He cared about her—a lot. More than he'd ever cared for a woman, even the one he'd planned on marrying. Cady fascinated him, captivated him, in a way he couldn't quite wrap his head around.

The office party was for him, not for her. He needed to see for himself that this Charles guy was as harmless as Cady said he was. He needed to know that Cady was treated with the respect she deserved. She deserved respect. She deserved a man who would take care of her and appreciate her for what she was. Amazing, sexy, untamed and fiercely loyal.

"Patton?" she asked, her eyes searching.

"Why are you so dead set against me taking you?" he asked, deciding evasion was the best course of action.

She sighed, shaking her head. She slid her fingers through her hair, tucking her hair behind her ear. He'd never seen her so rattled. She looked exhausted.

"You okay?" he asked, wanting to touch her so badly he shoved his hands in his pockets.

She looked at him, her mouth opening then closing. She nodded. "How's the case going?"

He shook his head. "Long week." A week of sleepless nights, convoluted files, dead-end tips and thoughts of Cady.

That seemed to irritate her all over again, her posture going rigid.

What had he said? His gaze swept her face, lingering on the tilt of her lips, the shadows under her eyes. "I owe you dinner. Tomorrow? Before the party?"

"Owe me?" she snapped, reaching for the car door handle. "Dammit, you don't *owe* me—"

"I want to take you to dinner," he all but growled.

She froze, staring at him. "Patton, are…are you asking me on a date? Is that what this is about?"

He stepped closer, unable to resist the pull between them. He needed to touch her. "If I am?"

She shook her head, but there was the hint of a smile on her lips. "I'd say it's a bad idea."

"That hasn't stopped us so far," he murmured, moving another step closer. Her scent hit him. "God, you smell good."

Her eyes went round and her breath grew unsteady. "You are the most exasperating man I know," she whispered.

He smiled. "Good to know." He reached up, tucking her hair behind her ear.

"N-no." She leaned away from him, but not before he saw the shudder that racked her slight frame.

He frowned. "No?" He was losing sight of the goal here. Being close to Cady did that, fogged things up and knocked him off course.

"The party's at seven. So there won't be time for us to get dinner first," she explained.

He refused to smile or gloat. She may not be aware that she'd just accepted he was her date tomorrow, but he was. And he was…happy. Aching for her, but happy. He cleared his throat. "Do I wear a suit?"

She nodded. "Patton, I don't know if I can do this." Her sudden change of topic spoke volumes. She was worrying over this, their plan.

He glanced at his mother's house. But Bianca and Cady's conversation replayed through his mind. Maybe he'd figure a way to learn more on their date. "It's the right thing to do, Cady. You know it. I know it."

She pulled open the car door. "My place, six thirty. Please don't be late."

"I won't." He held the door as he added, "You look pretty."

She tilted her head. "You have a nice ass."

He laughed. "Thanks."

She climbed into the car, giving him a heart-stopping view of her legs. He shook his head, closing his eyes and sighing deeply before closing her car door. She rolled down her window, saying, "You know this—we—are about sex, right? I mean it's great sex, but... It's still just sex." She shrugged and pulled away from the curb.

He stood there, frowning after her car. There was no denying that was how they'd started, but things had changed—for him. That was why he'd forced himself from her bed. He'd waited, her admission filling him with an emotion he was hesitant to name. The longer he lay there, the longer she stayed in that bathroom, the more he understood. She was panicking, she needed space. He didn't want to leave. He'd wanted to hold her close and sleep, to wake up with her, to be with her. If he'd stayed... He hadn't. And he regretted it.

Now she was leaving, going who knows where. Possibly with someone. Was it the someone she'd been talking to Bianca about? He frowned. No, he didn't want to know that. He pushed through the back gate, smiling as

Mikey ran around him in circles, dropping a ball at his feet and waiting expectantly. Patton picked up the ball.

"What was that?" Zach asked. "Seriously."

Patton tossed the ball and looked at his little brother. "What?"

Zach glanced over his shoulder at Bianca. "I know you're my big brother and you value your privacy but—"

"But?" Patton waited, throwing the ball Mikey had returned.

"Cady's Bianca's best friend. Guess I feel a sense of responsibility for her now that Bianca's clued me in on how crappy her childhood was and how terrible her parents are."

Patton nodded. No argument there.

Zach paused. "She told you?"

Patton looked at him.

Zach stepped closer. "So what's going on?"

Patton threw the ball again. "Nothing," he answered then changed course. "What's the plan with Bianca's shop? After you're married, I mean. Will she sell it so she can go with you when you're traveling a couple of weeks a month?

Zach frowned. "That shop is her dream. She's got two people on the payroll, people who count on her for their livelihood. I'm not going to ask her to give that up."

Patton nodded. Did Zach know she was in monetary trouble? "And your dream of traveling the world? Your high-paying, high-stress career? Are you shelving that?"

Zach sighed. "What are you getting at?"

"We've been talking about the wedding so much we hadn't had a chance to talk about your life afterward."

He paused, taking the ball from Mikey. "And the challenges your conflicting careers might bring."

"Shit, Patton," he whispered. "Is it that hard for you to be happy for me? I'd like to think having Bianca as part of the family is a good thing."

"You have to admit it's all pretty damn quick, Zach." He threw the ball, the questions spilling out before he could stop them. "What do you know about Bianca? Her family?"

"Are you serious?" Zach asked. "I'm the one with the past. She's…" He shook his head. "You know what? Forget it. I'm going to enjoy the rest of my evening."

Patton watched his brother stalk across the yard. He watched the concern on Bianca's face as she took Zach's hand. Zach wrapped his arm about her waist and whispered something in her ear, making her smile. He wanted to believe she loved his brother, that she had no ulterior motives. But until he learned all there was to know about Bianca, he would do his best to hold off any judgment.

Patton's phone rang.

Thirty minutes later, Patton stood amidst twisted metal and burning tires. An officer had attempted to pull over a trailer with its rear light out—completely unaware of the high-speed chase and multicar pile-up that would result. Two injured cops, a family of five whose minivan was struck and a motorcyclist who couldn't avoid the resulting debris were all en route to the local hospital.

Patton had been called in because of the trailer. It had been altered to manufacture meth; the walls and floors were permeated with the residue of the chemical burn off. Other than the smell and stains, there was no hardware or supplies for making the drug. The perps were probably on the way to dump it somewhere.

It was going to be a long night.

The highway was narrowed to one lane so the evidence processing could begin. Then taping off, photographing and marking the accident's path.

Nights like this he missed Russ most. He'd had one of those engaging personalities, keeping everyone smiling—even when they were working in the early hours of the morning with no light, honking horns and a feeling of defeat. His little brother had been a good cop. Until he wasn't a good cop anymore.

There were times he wished he could go back. Go back and confront his brother, try to get him to come clean. Try to get him some help before that night…

He was on the scene until the sun was up. On his way to the station, he stopped by his place long enough to grab a suit and throw his toiletries in a travel bag. He wouldn't have time to come home and get ready, so he'd clean up at the station before heading to Cady's.

The station was in chaos when he arrived, so he jumped in. Between last night's accident and two other ongoing cases, the background check he'd run on Bianca, her employees and close family members was the last thing on his mind. But when an email popped up saying the files were in his box and they needed to be returned ASAP, he stopped and stared at the screen, torn. His box was overflowing, but he could see the thick manila packet poking out. He slid it free and laid it on his desk, tapping the sealed top. Once he'd read this information, there was no going back. He opened the envelope, pulled out two files and leaned back in his chair. Of course, he didn't expect anyone to have a record…

He was wrong. Landon McCall was her delivery boy. He had a juvenile record of petty theft and shoplifting at three separate businesses. He'd worked it off through hours of community service and letters of recommendation. Patton skimmed over them, then flipped the page. As an adult, McCall had one prior—for check tampering. So Bianca was giving Landon another chance… Because she was big hearted or she didn't know?

He sighed, tucked the information back into the file and moved on to the next.

Bianca Garza. A DWI six year ago. She'd been sentenced to a one-year probation, paid a two-thousand dollar fine, had to attend a slew of education classes, served eighty hours of community service and had her license revoked for two years. He ran a hand over his face then skimmed through the rest of her file. Nothing else…in this file. That didn't mean Bianca didn't have other secrets.

He glanced at the clock. It was six fifteen. He was late.

10

CADY WAS PUTTING her earrings on when she heard a knock on her door. She glanced at the clock. It was six thirty-four. She ran down the hall and opened the door, her temper fizzling out at the delectable sight he presented. "You're not ready," she murmured.

His plaid shirt was untucked and open—baring his incredible torso and rendering her speechless. His jeans were unbuttoned, the top of his boxers and the dark line of hair that ran down from his belly button making her instantly, achingly aroused. She blinked, resisting the urge to run her fingers along the rock-hard abs he displayed and forcing her attention up. He looked exhausted, sporting a thick stubble on his jaw and shadows under his eyes. Even exhausted he looked good enough to eat.

"Work ran late." He held up his hanging bag. "I need five minutes and a shower."

"A shower?" Her mind went crazy with the possibilities. She'd need more than five minutes. And then they'd be late. "Now?" she asked, stepping aside so he could come in.

He stopped inside, his gaze locking with hers… He might be tired, but he wasn't dead. The flare of want in his eyes had her wetting her lower lip with the tip of her tongue.

"Cady…" He growled in warning. "Keep that up and it'll be at least ten minutes."

"Ten minutes? Wow." She grinned, arching a brow. "What did you have in mind?" She ran her pointer finger along the waist of his boxers. So what if they were late?

He shook his head, closing his eyes. He sucked in a deep breath, backing away from her touch. "You're all dressed up and ready to go. I don't want to…mess up your hair." He swallowed.

"You don't?" she asked.

"I want to. I will. After," he promised. His gaze swept over her again. He swallowed. "How about a cup of coffee?"

"Coffee coming up." She grinned. "You know the way."

"Thanks." He nodded, his eyes traveling over her. He groaned, cupping her chin and kissing her. She parted her lips, inviting him in. He groaned again, breaking the kiss. "Five minutes…maybe ten." He shook his head again then brushed past her and down the hall to her bedroom.

She watched him go, appreciating the view of his arms as he shrugged out of his shirt. She had it bad. She blew out a slow breath, staring after the man who continued to knock her off her feet.

He paused, winked and disappeared into her room.

Her bedroom. The room she'd kept to herself, her own little oasis—no men allowed—until Patton. And after he'd left her, she remembered why she'd never brought anyone else back here. It was because it *was* Patton that it had hurt to find her bed empty. She'd never felt so alone and vulnerable.

She busied herself in the kitchen, making a cup of strong coffee. Sexy or not, she could tell he was wiped out. If he'd been on the job all night, who knew when he'd eaten last? It took no effort to make him a roast beef sandwich—protein would do him some good. She added an apple and a handful of almonds to the plate and carried the coffee and snack to her room.

The bedroom door was ajar, so she nudged it wide with her hip. She couldn't help but smile at the neatly folded jeans and shirt that sat on the chair in the corner. His boots rested underneath it—all neat and orderly. She heard the water shut off and called out, "Coffee's ready."

He pulled the door open, releasing a cloud of steam into her bedroom. She tried not to react, but it was hopeless. He was all wet and sexy as hell with his hair flopping into his eyes. He reached for the coffee with one hand. The other held his towel—dangerously low—around his hips. "Thanks."

"Are you up for this?" she asked, trying not to ogle while offering him the plate. "I can think of other things we could do tonight."

He took the plate, smiling at the food, before leveling her with a hard stare. "Any of them have the potential to forward your career?" He smiled broadly.

She smiled, perching on the edge of her bed. "Look who's being all gentlemanly tonight."

"A rarity, I know." His attention wandered up her legs. "That's what you're wearing?" his voice was thick.

"What's wrong with it?" She glanced down at her

gray cocktail dress. It was a sheath dress, nothing too fancy, but there was a slight shimmer through the fabric. It draped nicely on her shoulders and hit midknee. And it made her blond stripe pop.

"Nothing." He shook his head. "You look...sexy as hell."

"*I* look sexy?" She shook her head, nodding at him and his towel. "I was going for professional or demure or classy."

"To me, you look sexy." He grinned.

She smiled, savoring his compliment. "Another cup?" she asked, watching him tear into the sandwich.

"That would be great," he said after swallowing.

She grinned, appreciating his enthusiasm. "I got word today that one of the partners from the Japanese firm we're working with might be attending tonight."

Patton finished the nuts then bit into the apple. He swallowed before asking, "That's kind of a big deal, isn't it?"

"It is," she agreed, her eyes wandering to the breadth of his chest, his muscled shoulders and thick arms. Her mouth went dry at the sight of him. She'd always had a healthy sexual appetite. But Patton had made her insatiable.

"So this is good?"

"Hmm?" she asked, distracted by how low the towel had slipped.

"Cady," he ground out.

She stood. "What?"

He crossed his arms over his chest, making her giggle. "Thank you for the food."

She wanted to tug that towel free and stare at the rest

of him. He stood, watching her. "You'll need energy… for later."

His jaw clenched, and the throb between her legs intensified. The apartment buzzer sounded. "That'll be the car," she murmured.

"The car?" he repeated.

"My boss sent it." She frowned, allowing herself one more look before giving up. "So hurry."

"Yes, ma'am." He nodded as he went back into the bathroom. She lingered, watching him open his overnight bag and pull out his shaving kit. There was something very nice about him being here, getting ready, talking to her and her taking care of him. Having him here didn't crowd her or irritate her. He…fit. She ached with a different kind of want.

"More coffee coming up," she murmured as she hurried from the bedroom. She made another cup of coffee, her attention wandering back down the hallway to her room.

No one had ever cared about her need for success— except for her. Her parents were indifferent. They didn't understand Cady's drive to be better, to keep her edge. But Patton was turning down what would undoubtedly be a night of incredible sex to support her and her career. Not that they wouldn't make up for it later, but… Her heart felt full and heavy with all the things she shouldn't feel for him.

Tonight she needed to prove to her boss that she was the best candidate for the promotion. She checked her reflection in the mirror for smudges, but she was good. She smoothed her hair, grabbed Patton's cup of coffee and headed back down the hallway to her bedroom.

Patton was buttoning up his shirt, clean shaven, damp hair and so gorgeous Cady felt her insides quiver.

"Thanks." He took the cup, his pale gaze lingering on her. "Still think you look sexy."

"Nothing says sexy like a modest neckline and midknee length." She teased, watching him tie his tie. "Long night?"

"Never got to bed last night." He shrugged into his coat. "Had an incident on the highway and got called in right after you left."

"God, Patton. This isn't that important—"

And then he was kissing her. It was a soft kiss, one that lingered in just the right way. "It is…so stop trying to tempt me into taking you to bed. You ready?" he asked against her lips.

She stared up at him, fighting down the words that bubbled up inside of her. "Yes."

He finished his coffee. "Let's go." He took her hand and led her back down the hallway and out the front door. "How's work? Everything ready for the software run this weekend?"

She glanced at him, locking her door behind them. She'd been talking to Bianca about her weekend plans, not him. "You eavesdrop often?" she asked.

"Pretty much. Hazards of the job, I guess. Always listening," he admitted.

What else had he heard? She swallowed down her nerves and focused on the question. "I've done everything I can do. Charles seems to have done his part. Now all we can do is sit back and watch." She shrugged as she entered the elevator.

The doors shut and she looked at him. "You clean up well, Detective."

"Still intimidating?" he asked, glancing at her. "If the need arises."

She grinned. "It won't. Poor Charles."

His gaze met hers, setting off all sorts of tingles. "We rode an elevator on our first date, didn't we?"

She arched a brow, unable to deny the impact those memories had upon her. "Are you asking because you don't remember? Or because you're wanting to get me flustered?"

He turned toward her, stepping closer. "Would you?"

"Would I what?" she murmured, unable to move.

"Get flustered?" he asked.

She shook her head, knowing her voice would give her away. She was beyond flustered, but he didn't need to know it. He had the advantage here. She had no idea how he felt about her...or why he'd left her apartment when she'd taken her marathon shower. She studied him. The slight tightening of his jaw, the rasp in his breathing and the undeniable heat in his eyes. His hunger for her was the ultimate turn-on. As if she could get any more turned on.

She tore her gaze from his, ignoring the throb of her body, and watched the numbers count down on the elevator. Lust she understood. The rest, feelings and doubt and conflict, she didn't. Add in the whole Bianca and Zach mess and she knew they had no chance outside the bedroom. Better to keep it simple, enjoy the sizzle between them, instead of letting her emotions get in the way. The elevator opened to her building's lobby. The limo was parked out front. She glanced back to find him staring at her butt. "Patton."

"What?" he asked, following her slowly. "I'm appreciating the view."

She laughed. She couldn't help it.

Once they climbed into the limo, Cady knew she was in trouble. His fingers grasped hers, turning over her hand so he could stroke the inside of her wrist. She shuddered, the stroke of his touch radiating. She had no idea her arm was an erogenous zone, but damn, he had her aching. She didn't know how much more she could take, but the drive wasn't that far.

"Patton..." Her protest was more plea than anything else.

He lifted her hand, kissing her skin, raking his nose along her arm to the bend of her elbow. "I like the way you smell," he whispered hoarsely.

She pressed her palm to his face. "You plan on seducing me in a limo?" She hissed as his tongue flicked between her fingers. "Isn't that a little too cliché?"

"No." His lips descended on hers, softly, lightly. "I don't have cliché fantasies."

"Fantasy?" she asked. Far be it from her to deny a man his sexual fantasies.

His fingers traced the edge of her skirt, eliciting a full-body shiver from her. As his hand slipped beneath the fabric of her dress, his mouth latched on to her earlobe. He was two seconds away from discovering she'd left her panties in her apartment—when the limo came to a stop.

"That was fast," she muttered, grappling with her disappointment.

"Too fast," he said against her neck. He groaned, putting some space between them.

She glanced out the window, staring at the hotel. It was *the* hotel—the one they'd stumbled into that first night together, too caught up in one another to care where they'd ended up—as long as there was a bed.

"Awesome," she whispered, the instant thrill of memory warm upon her skin.

"Déjà vu," he murmured.

She cocked an eyebrow at him.

"That night's crystal clear." His voice was gravel.

She looked at him then. "So you *were* trying to get me flustered earlier?"

The hunger of his gaze made her insides melt. She knew this evening had the potential to be complicated. He was the first date she'd ever brought to an office party. And while she knew the only threat Charles posed was to her promotion, Patton thought he was there to defend her honor. Not that having him at her side was a bad thing. If anything, it might help. Mr. Hembrecht was all about family and stability. Maybe showing up with an upstanding member of the community could work in her favor. If she could only get a handle on this…this crazy, electric, pulsing connection that made the air around them hum, it might just turn out to be a nice evening.

The valet opened the door, forcing them out of the car, "Good evening."

"You ready?" Patton asked.

She nodded.

"Maybe we can take the long way home," he teased.

She laughed as she took the valet's hand and slid from the car. She was still smiling when Patton hooked her arm through his and led her into the lobby. Try as she might, she was hyper in tune with this man. When he released her arm to let her go ahead of him, his hand rested on the base of her spine. His scent, clean and musky, wrapped around her—making her dizzy. It was going to be a long night.

As they reached the ballroom, she turned to Patton and smoothed the front of his shirt. "Here we go, Detective."

"Anything I need to know?" His hand took hers. "Or should I just stand here and be your arm candy?"

She burst out laughing, totally thrown by his sudden humor.

"Cady?" Her boss, Mr. Ronald Hembrecht, stood just inside the dimly lit ballroom. "You look lovely."

She accepted his handshake. "Thank you, Mr. Hembrecht. I'd like to introduce you to Patton Ryan. Patton, Mr. Hembrecht—"

"Ronald, please, Cady." Mr. Hembrecht shook his head. "Very nice to meet you, Patton." He looked back and forth between them. Cady could only imagine the barrage of questions she'd have directed at her on Monday morning.

Patton smiled at her then shook her boss's hand. "Pleasure to meet you. I know Cady enjoys her work— that says a lot about who's in charge."

Mr. Hembrecht's smile grew. "I agree. A happy employee is a loyal employee." He regarded Cady then. "Cady is a huge asset to the company, one I want to keep on my payroll."

"She's a catch," Patton agreed, taking her hand again.

Cady glanced at their hands, pleased at the warmth and support that simple touch provided her.

"Hey, Cady." Charles joined them. "You look great. Charles Hembrecht," he said, offering his hand to Patton.

"Patton Ryan." Patton shook his hand. "Nice to meet the man behind the texts."

Cady stared up at him, horrified. But Patton was smiling, at ease. By all appearances, he was teasing—making small talk. But she knew better. She squeezed the hand she held tightly.

"Guilty." Charles smiled even as he glanced at his father.

Mr. Hembrecht glanced back and forth between Cady and his son. "Texts? After-hours?"

Charles blew out a deep breath.

"Just while he was getting situated," Cady filled in. "It's a demanding job."

Mr. Hembrecht wasn't pleased, but he was a true professional. With one quick look at his son, he conveyed disapproval. "Indeed," Mr. Hembrecht murmured. "What do you do, Patton?"

"He's a detective," she offered, eager to steer the conversation in a new direction. "Like his father before him."

"Talk about a demanding job." Charles was clearly assessing Patton.

"It has its moments," Patton agreed.

"Thank you for your service," Mr. Hembrecht said. "It's a noble profession, one that doesn't get the respect it deserves."

Patton smiled, nodding his head at her boss.

"Or the required breaks that the corporate world gets. Talk about dedication. How many hours have you gone without sleep?" she asked.

He shook his head. "A few," he admitted, grinning.

"Then he must be equally dedicated to you," Mr. Hembrecht offered.

Cady felt the weight of Patton's gaze on her but resisted the urge to look at him. She was mortified to feel the heat in her cheeks. More troubling was the nervous giddiness that welled inside her, pressing against her chest and tightening her throat.

"Cady, I took a call from Japan this afternoon. No one was able to get away," Mr. Hembrecht continued, "but the chairman said he would be touching base with you Monday."

Cady nodded, relaxing somewhat. "Let's hope everything runs without a hitch."

Mr. Hembrecht nodded. "It will. I have every confidence in you. You two go get something to drink. Have a nice time."

The night went surprisingly well. She hadn't known what, exactly, to expect. But this Patton—this charming, easygoing guy—was pretty much the ideal date. He shook hands, made small talk and took care of her. When Meg from Human Resources got a look at him, she gave Cady the thumbs-up. When her team met him, she watched their reactions with interest. Overall, Patton seemed to be the most exciting thing to happen to this year's party.

The problem was, he was the most exciting thing to happen to her—ever. And, as much as she didn't want to admit it, she no longer had a choice. She accepted the terrifying truth. She was in love with Patton Ryan.

PATTON'S ATTENTION FOLLOWED CADY. Watching her was revealing, not just because of her actions but because of the reactions of those around her. People responded to her, warmed to her. She had that spark, the thing that drew people in and made them want her attention. He was careful; he didn't want Cady to think he was fixated on her. He sighed. Who was he trying to kid? He *was* fixated on her… No, dammit, it was way past that. He wasn't just interested. He cared about her.

Why else was he here? Cady could handle a flirtatious coworker. After meeting Charles, he knew he had nothing to worry about. It was time to come clean. He'd wanted to come, to be a part of Cady's life—since she'd invaded almost every aspect of his.

Once he accepted his feelings, he decided he might as well go with it and enjoy Cady—her energy and spirit. She knew how to work a room, radiating a sexy-as-hell confidence he couldn't help but admire. More than that, she was smart. He saw how respected she was, not just by those who worked for her or with her, but by her superiors, as well. They found Mr. Hembrecht and two other partners, and Cady spent the better part of thirty minutes explaining a new interface she was considering. She knew her stuff. Confidence and competence in one sexy package.

Her presentation was impressive. He didn't understand a lot of the lingo she was using, but he understood the concept. Security. Cady's job was keeping computer information secure. If there was a glitch, it was her job to find it and fix it. And the new programs she'd put into place had reduced the security breaches and hacks to their clients' databases by a third.

When her eyes met his, he saw the thrill of pride she was experiencing. He knew how that felt, to be proud of the job you'd done. To be confident and in control. She was amazing—and gorgeous.

He wasn't sure which was more rewarding, that Cady was as celebrated as she was or that he was the first guy she'd ever brought to *any* office function. Something that was repeated by pretty much everyone he was introduced to. Either way, he was having a surprisingly good time. Even if part of him was ready to go home and face-plant in bed—preferably Cady's bed.

"Tired?" she asked.

"Nope, I'm good."

Her gaze searched his face. "I'm tired... And starving. We've made the rounds. Since I don't need to be here for our Japanese client, there's no point in sticking around. We can go to a drive-through, grab some burgers and hit the hay."

"Burgers?" he asked. "You're speaking my language."

"If you think I've done my job?" she asked, staring up at him. "Have I shown the top brass how amazing I am? That I'm the only one for this promotion and they need me?"

"I think so. I'd give you the promotion." He smiled down at her.

"So, you're satisfied?"

He leaned closer. "I'm nowhere near satisfied."

He loved the sound of her shocked laughter. "You have something in mind?"

He nodded, his gaze dipping to her chest.

"Tonight, you're mine."

She shivered, her breath escaping on a shaky exhale. "I am?"

He pulled her closer, bending his head to whisper, "I'd like to drag you out of here and get things started... In the limo. Unless you have any problems with that?"

She shook her head, her gaze caught up in his. "That's not very gentlemanly of you."

"So tonight you're in the mood for a gentleman?"

He watched her eyes widen and her breath hitch. He loved the way her lips parted and her cheeks colored.

"I can't tell if you're teasing me or propositioning me," her voice was husky.

He tucked her blond streak behind her ear, his thumb brushing along her jawline in the process. "Guess I need to work on my proposals then."

Meg interrupted them, grabbing Cady's arm. "Cady," her voice slurred slightly. "Did you hear? Rumor has it Charles got the job."

Patton took Cady's hand in his. He kept his mouth shut, knowing he'd have plenty of time to defuse the rumor bomb Meg was dropping. Rumors and alcohol were never a good mix.

"I'm so sorry, Cady. You're the one that's worked your ass off—covering for him. We all know it. If you're not the boss, maybe it's time to find a new place to work," Meg kept on, her words running together. Patton took in her dilated pupils and flushed skin. Meg had drunk more than her fair share of the bright yellow drinks she'd been enjoying all evening.

"Meg, come on. Charles isn't a bad guy," Cady argued. "We'll see what happens, okay?"

"You're so sweet…" Meg sighed, glancing at Patton. "And you're so lucky." She raked her finger along his chest, then giggled. "Do you have a brother?"

"One single. A few cousins, too." Patton grinned at her then. "You need to take a cab home."

Meg winked. "All right."

"Promise?" Cady asked, shooting Patton a glance.

"Sure." Meg swayed forward. "No problem."

Patton understood Cady's look. He didn't like it, but he understood. Instead of hot limo sex, he was going to help Cady get Meg safely home. "We'll give you a ride," he offered.

Cady's smile was blinding. "Yeah, come on. We're leaving anyway."

"I don't want to be a party pooper," Meg argued even as she slid her arm through his and leaned against him heavily. "Get in the way of any…plans." She bobbed her eyebrows, looking between them and smiling.

Patton glanced at Cady. "Don't worry, Meg. Only plan I can count on is a burger."

Meg looked confused, but Cady burst out laughing as she said, "Come on."

"Better be a good burger," he added as he steered Meg across the ballroom while Cady made their good-byes. He was having a hell of a time keeping Meg up-right as they maneuvered up the stairs.

He nodded his farewells and watched Cady make a graceful exit. If she was upset over what Meg said, he couldn't see it. It was only after they managed to get Meg into the limo, where she proceeded to pass out on Cady's shoulder, that he saw her smile slip.

_11_

CADY COULDN'T SEEM to sit still. She was so mad…she wanted to scream, to yell, to fight. She stared blindly out the window, the shops and buildings a blur as the limo navigated the streets. She glanced at Patton, the already accelerated rate of her heart picking up. She'd stare at him. Staring at Patton would take her mind off work, the promotion and her profound disappointment in Mr. Hembrecht. Patton was gorgeous and a nice distraction.

A gorgeous man who'd had no problem carrying Meg up the stairs to her apartment. A gorgeous man who fed Meg's meowing cat while Cady helped Meg get into bed. He'd done it all without a single complaint.

Tonight, you're mine… His words were the most thrilling thing she'd ever heard. Her heart thumped, warmth pooling in the pit of her stomach.

He glanced at her. "You okay?"

She hadn't said anything since they left—she couldn't. And now she was even more mixed up. "Yeah."

"Mad?" His voice was low.

"I am. I'm trying not to be, but I am." She gripped the edge of her seat, her anger bubbling up. "Why the hell would Hembrecht promote him? I mean, besides the fact that Charles is his son. He's incapable of doing the job. He has no idea what's going on—unless I explain it to him." She sat back in her chair, sighing. "It really pisses me off."

"It should." Patton's deep voice rolled over her. "But all you have to go on is Meg's story. And, considering how drunk she was, I'd hold off on reacting." His hand found hers in the dark. "Glad you have the weekend to think things over."

He was right. He was supersexy, supersupportive… and they had some time to kill.

"Enough talking," she said, sliding across the seat.

He responded in an instant. His hands gripped her hips, facing him—on his lap. She felt the length of his erection and smiled.

"Who knew a limo was such a turn-on for you?" she murmured before pressing her lips to his.

His lips parted, the tip of his tongue tracing her lower lip. He wanted her. He'd wanted her from the minute she'd opened her apartment door. No, he'd wanted her from the moment she sat across from him at that restaurant—that very first night.

The limo stopped, and they both looked out the window. They were at the restaurant.

Patton sighed then laughed.

The driver's voice filled the cab. "The drive-through is too narrow for the car."

"We'll go in," Patton said, tucking her hair behind her ear.

She frowned as she slid from his lap. "You're no fun."

"A man's got to eat. And sleep," he argued, helping

her from the car. He took her hand in his as they walked across the parking lot to the local gourmet burger joint.

"Any new leads on your case?" she asked.

"Looks like the mom is willing to cooperate. Hopefully, it's enough to keep her family together. I believe she didn't have anything to do with the fire." He shrugged. "But without evidence or useful info, what I believe doesn't matter."

She was watching him closely, studying him. "How long can you keep going without sleep?" Cady asked as Patton placed their to-go order.

"Longest I've been up is almost seventy-two hours. But I was only good for about sixty of those, the rest was autopilot." He paused. "Drink?"

"No, thanks." She faced him, exploring every rugged feature of his face. "Only sixty." She laughed, shaking her head. "What was the case?"

"A stakeout a few years back. The neighborhood was hot, so we couldn't leave often. And we were understaffed—like always—someone had to stay. Since I don't have a family to go home to, I volunteer."

No family. She frowned. She'd seen his family. It was gargantuan—and more than a little intimidating. Cady picked back up, "What about Mikey? He's your family."

"He loves my mom," he shot back. "You've seen her yard, it's big. And she has a pool. Mikey is a true lab, he loves the water. My yard—" he paused, shrugging "—it's still a...work in progress."

"Meaning you bought a fixer? This doesn't surprise me."

"I did," he agreed, grinning at her. "Probably the biggest mistake I ever made, considering how little time I have for fixing things. But it's a great house."

Once they were back on the road, they chatted about the repairs and remodel ideas he had for his place. She'd never taken the time to invest in her apartment. She had everything she needed, considering how little she was there. Considering the only two rooms she regularly used were her kitchen and her bedroom suite, she could probably downsize and be just as happy.

Further proof that they were different. He saw his huge extended family as no family. But she knew what it meant to actually have no family. His idea of home was a place to put his stamp on, to renovate and build. Her idea of home was a place to relax in, without worrying about old wiring or bad plumbing. It's not as if she needed more proof that they weren't meant to be together. And even though she didn't want a relationship, she did want—did love—Patton. "I'd like to see your place sometime," she spoke without thinking, leading him up to her apartment.

She wasn't a fan of not knowing. She was a planner. Details and structure with a clear-cut goal in mind. But since she'd met Patton, she'd been in a constant state of confusion.

She fumbled with the keys in the lock then. The last thing she needed was to get more involved in his life. Any of the Ryans really, as nice as the family was. Once the wedding was over—one way or the other— life would get back to normal. Normal as in without Patton.

"I'll take you by tomorrow," he offered, reaching around her to open the door for her.

She closed her eyes, enjoying the warmth of his chest against her back. His arm slipped around her waist, his hand closing over hers to turn the key in the lock. She smiled as he pressed a kiss to the base of her neck.

"I thought you were hungry." She hurried into her apartment, his kiss lingering at the nape of her neck.

His eyes followed her, determined.

She put her hands on her hips. "Since the limo fell through, the only proposition left on the table tonight is eating hamburgers."

He closed the door behind him, placed the bag of food on the table and pressed the tabletop with both hands. He stood back, nodding. "The table's too hard for much else anyway."

She giggled—she couldn't help it. The flare of hunger in his eyes kept her rooted in place. But something changed his mind, because instead of reaching for her, he made himself at home in the kitchen. He pulled out two plates and a couple of napkins.

"Beer's in the fridge," she offered—still a little breathless.

He grabbed two from the fridge and met her at the table. She put the food on the plates while he opened the beers.

"Need me to prop you up on anything?" she asked, taking in his heavy-lidded eyes.

He took a long swig of the beer, his eyes locking with hers. "Define anything?"

She rolled her eyes, pulling the pickles off her burger.

He paused, watching her. Then did the same. "Me neither."

She was smiling when she took her first bite.

They ate in companionable silence. She only finished half, but enjoyed every last French fry. He inhaled his food, every bite. And had a second beer.

"When did you eat last?" she asked.

"The snack you made me," he said. "Other than that…at my mother's house." He sat back, his gaze searching hers with a fiery intensity. He shook his head—jaw locked and nostrils flared.

"Done?" she asked, her pulse picking up.

But he didn't say anything. Instead his gaze stayed fixed on hers, turning her insides molten. She pressed her legs together, the throb undeniable. His eyes blazed with want. For her. Now.

"Patton—" she blew out a long, slow breath. It wasn't just sex anymore. It wasn't falling into a hotel room or hooking up in a limo and watching him drive away. It was him, here—invading her personal space and making her vulnerable.

Yes, she wanted him like crazy. But she loved him. Knowing that made her consider the aftereffects of another night in his arms. She didn't know what to expect—or hope for. If she was smart, she'd help him get his things together, wave him off and lock the door behind him. She should be strong and guard her heart… Instead she stood in front of him. "Stay," she murmured, the word so thick it was barely decipherable.

He sat forward, his hands clasping her hips and pulling her between his legs. He pressed his face against her stomach as his hands slid up the back of her thighs. Her fingers ran through his thick black hair, holding him to her.

"I won't pretend I don't want you, Cady," his voice was thick, "but things are getting…out of hand."

He had no idea… Did he?

Her fingers tightened in his hair, pulling his head back. She stooped, pressing her lips to his and leaning into him. His hands gripped the hem of her dress, tugging it up and over her head. She tossed it aside and unhooked her bra, letting it drop.

He groaned, realizing she wore no panties. His eyes flashed when they met hers. His hands tugged her closer, cupping one breast and drawing it to his mouth.

She arched into his touch, loving the stroke of his tongue on her skin. The brush of his breath on her nipple made her quiver. When he sucked her nipple deep into his mouth, Cady moaned. It didn't take much to make her crazy, to have her aching for all of him. It was... Patton. Just Patton. She gave in, letting sensation take over. She fumbled with his pants, tugging him free before he pulled her onto him. She straddled him, taking him deep—loving the feel of him, the pressure. He was in no hurry. His hold on her set a slow and steady pace and drove her mad with his leisurely rhythm.

"Cady." The word was a broken whisper.

She opened her eyes, gasping for breath.

He kissed her, softly. His hands brushed her hair back from her face, but his eyes never left hers. He cradled her face, his gaze holding hers—searching hers—as he moved into her.

It was too intense, too...much. She wanted to look away, to sever the connection between them. But she couldn't. Something in his gaze held her captive. Her body responded instantly, shaking with the force of her release. She cried out, her hands gripping his shoulders through the fabric of his dress shirt.

He kissed her then, wrapping one arm around her waist and holding her to him. His whole body stiffened as he held her tightly in place. She felt the power of his release, the clenching of his muscles, as he muffled his groan against her neck.

When his hold eased, she sat back. "You must be ready for bed."

His gaze was wary. "Want me to go?"

She frowned, not wanting him to go. "You can." She swallowed, so nervous she could barely say, "Or you can stay…tonight."

She hadn't expected him to look like that, to smile like that. But it was a thing of beauty.

"SCRAMBLED, FRIED—what's your pleasure?" Patton asked, sliding a cup of coffee to Cady.

Her hair was mussed, and she wore an oversize T-shirt with the picture of some band he'd never heard of on the front. "Oh, God, are you a morning person?" she asked, accepting the coffee with a sleepy grin.

He shrugged. Not normally, but this morning he was. This morning he'd woken up feeling pretty damn good. Maybe it was because he'd needed the sleep. Or maybe it was because he'd woken up to Cady's head on his chest, her hand resting on his side. He'd lain there for almost an hour, dozing, enjoying the way she fit against him.

"What time is it?" she asked, wiping her eyes and yawning. She was adorable.

"Nine." He grinned.

Her eyes popped open. "But, we're supposed to meet them in thirty minutes," she hurried back down the hallway, carrying her coffee.

"No breakfast?" he called after her, cracking two eggs into a frying pan.

"Surprise me," she called back. "Thanks for the coffee."

He scrambled some eggs and fried some bacon, considering his options. Now that he knew Bianca had secrets, he needed to find out how big—and how many—there were. Cady was the best way to do that. But now that this had happened, he didn't know where to start. Hell, he didn't even know what this was. Except he liked it. He liked sleeping next to her, touching her in the night—knowing she was next to him. And waking up with her... It was all good. He was beginning to suspect they might be good together.

But family came first. Stopping this wedding came first. He had to keep his eye on the prize and keep his family safe.

He sighed, digging through the pantry when she reappeared. He tried not to stare, but it was impossible. She looked soft, touchable, in her light-weight pale pink top and jeans. He watched her slide her feet into some strappy brown sandals so that her bright blue toenails were visible. She looked—was—utterly kissable.

"What?" she asked, putting sparkly hoops in each ear.

She was beautiful. It wasn't hard to say, but the words stuck in his throat. Instead he swallowed, asking, "Tortillas?"

"Don't have any. I've got low-fat sandwich rounds." She joined him, moving stuff around on the pantry shelves. "If they're still good."

"Sounds yummy." His sarcasm was hard to miss.

She laughed, nudging him with her hip. "Well... How about naan? It's good."

"Let's try it." He pulled the package out and crisped up the bread before rolling makeshift breakfast tacos.

She watched him, not saying a word. "Thanks."

He eyed the food. "You might not be all that thankful after you take the first bite." He inhaled his food and downed another cup of coffee while she finished hers.

He washed up quickly, still searching for the right way to shift the conversation to Bianca.

"It was good. Who knew?" she asked, grabbing her bag. She pressed a kiss to his cheek. "Thank you."

She headed toward the door before he could wrap his arms around her. Which was good. He didn't need any more distractions. And, when Cady was close, she was definitely a distraction. He grabbed his overnight bag and suit and held the door open for her.

"Thanks," she repeated, locking the door behind them. She glanced at him as they made their way down the hall and hit the elevator button. "Still tired? Did I keep you up?"

He glanced at her. He could have a hell of a time turning her words around. But now wasn't the time to tease or flirt. They didn't have much time this morning, and he needed answers. "Feeling pretty good this morning," he said as the elevator doors shut.

She looked at him, her expression stiffening. "Good." Her voice was tight. She was upset. Her hands fiddled with the straps of her purse. She shifted from one foot to the other.

What the hell had he done? Or said? This was why he was no good with women. He didn't understand them.

"I ordered the cake," she said suddenly. "The baby cake?"

He nodded. "Okay. Kimber is free for the shower, too."

"Kimber?" She looked at him.

"Zach's ex," he explained.

"Oh, right, the stripper." She grimaced.

"Anything else we can use?" he asked. "Something or someone from her past we could use—"

"No strippers in her past," Cady cut him off.

"It doesn't have to be a stripper," he argued. "We need more to break this up, Cady."

She stared at him for a long time. "She...she's been engaged before."

He paused, considering her words. "Once? Or several times?" he tried to keep his voice neutral.

Her brown eyes bore into his. She was deciding, he could tell. "More than once."

"What happened?" he asked.

The elevator doors opened in the garage. He had to convince her to ride with him, since he was finally getting somewhere. "I'll drive," he offered quickly. Before he could change his mind he added, "If we get there early enough, I'll grill us some steaks. You can see the house... Throw the ball for Mikey." What was he doing?

Her brown eyes met his, a rapid-fire shift of emotions crossing her face. A crease formed between her eyebrows then disappeared.

"You think about it," he interrupted. "I'll drive."

"Okay," she answered, following him to his truck.

He tried to shrug off the hurt her of her hesitation. Eye on the prize. He waited until he'd started the truck before asking, "What happened with Bianca's other engagements?"

Cady seemed to deflate in her seat. "You're going to overreact."

He glanced at her. "I am?"

"You don't understand her family," Cady explained. "How important her grandmother is. How they were raised."

"Why don't we start with what happened?" Patton asked, his stomach churning.

"You know Bibi's grandmother is a matchmaker?" Cady asked, not waiting for him to answer. "Well, for one thing, GG didn't match Bibi with any of the others."

"Any as in how many?"

But Cady didn't say anything.

He glanced at her. "Cady?"

"You were engaged. It didn't work out but that doesn't make you a bad person," she argued. "You thought you were in love with her when you proposed, though, didn't you?"

"I never said Bianca was a bad person," he murmured, hoping to dodge her last question. Had he loved Ellie? Yes, he'd loved her. But had he been in love with her? Did seeing her make him happy? Had being with her filled some void? Had he thought about her when they were apart? Or ached for her the way he ached for Cady? He swallowed. "What does this have to do with anything?"

"It means people make mistakes, even all-knowing police officers like you."

"Cady, you're twisting things around. My engagement to Ellie is different. Yes, I cared about her, but she broke it off before I could do it," he explained. "There were extenuating circumstances—"

"Such as?" Cady prodded.

"Russ died. My father had a heart attack. I was too busy to think about Ellie or our engagement. But Russ's death, my getting shot, my dad almost dying…was too much for her. I didn't blame her for ending it—I understood. Hell, I agreed with her."

Cady grew silent. He glanced her way to see her staring at him. "What?"

She shook her head, opening and closing her mouth. She sighed then said, "What about Bianca's extenuating circumstances?"

"You never answered my first question," he countered. "How many times has she been engaged?"

"Why does it matter?" she snapped.

He looked at her. "It shouldn't. So why aren't you telling me?"

"Three," she murmured.

"She's been engaged three times? And she broke it off with all of them because her grandmother didn't have *the* dream? The matchmaking thing?"

"No, Patton, there was more—"

"I sure as hell hope there is. Otherwise… Three times? We'd better be talking about some serious extenuating circumstances."

He saw Cady's eyes close, saw the furrow that creased her brow. "There are. You need to calm down and listen. I know it sounds—"

"It sounds crazy?" he asked, shaking his head. "I don't need to calm down. I need to talk to my brother."

"Patton—"

"Give me a minute," he bit out. The truck fell quiet while he processed this new information. Did Zach know about this? Or the DWI? "What about the DWI?" he asked.

Cady turned in her seat. "How did you know about that? Oh, you...you did a background check on her?" Her voice was high and pinched. "Did *Zach* ask you to check up on her? Or did you take this on yourself?" She waited, but he didn't say a thing. "How is that fair? We all have mistakes in our past, Patton. But not all of us have the resources to track it all down like you do."

He wasn't about to apologize for protecting his family. "I'm guessing the DWI is why Bianca doesn't drink?"

But Cady wasn't talking. And when he looked over at her, she was staring out the window—her arms crossed over her chest, red faced and breathing hard.

"You can be pissed at me, Cady, I get it. But you need to understand this isn't about attacking Bianca. I'm trying to stop this wedding, remember? The wedding we both disapprove of." He breathed deeply, his stomach churning. "Does Zach know this? About the DWI? And the engagements?"

"How can you say you're not attacking Bianca? You want to use her past to make her...her *unfit* to marry your brother." She shook her head, ignoring his questions. "Did he ask you to run the background check?"

"What does it matter, Cady? It's done." He shook his head. "Clearly, they don't know each other. They sure as hell shouldn't be getting married."

"And the best way to stop them is tear Bianca apart? It will destroy her, Patton. No matter what you think of her, she's a good person. Surely you can see that?" Her brown eyes were fixed on him, demanding some sort of concession. "She's been through so much—"

"We're talking about facts, Cady." He swallowed back the regret.

Cady's stare was hard, unblinking and cold. "Guess the cake and the stripper are overkill at this point, huh?"

"Cady…" But what could he say.

"What was I thinking? What were we doing?" She shook her head. "I'm such an idiot."

He heard the frustration in her voice and it tore at his chest. He was tempted to drive past Bianca's shop, to try to talk through things. But there was nothing to say. As much as he cared about Cady, he had an obligation to his brother—his family.

He pulled into the parking lot of Bianca's Jardin and turned off the truck.

"Do me one favor," her voice was soft, thick.

He didn't look at her. "What?"

"Don't do this publicly," she pleaded. "You don't know what she's been through. What her family has been through."

He glanced at her then, still reeling from everything he'd learned. "Cady, this is always what we'd planned on doing."

She shook her head. "Not like this." Her eyes were huge in her pale face.

"You really thought a cake mix-up and an ex-girlfriend would be enough?" he asked.

Her anger roared to life. "I don't know what I thought, Patton. I don't have a vast experience with this sort of thing. Yes, I wanted to stop this—to prevent them from getting hurt. But you're using information that's private. Damn you, Patton, you're making *me* betray Bianca."

"I'm making sure my brother knows the truth about the woman he's engaged to." He slammed his hand against the steering wheel. "Facts that my brother needs to know."

"Was this your plan all along?" She choked out the words. "Get to know the best friend. Soften me up. Charm me into bed. Make me fall for you. So you can get all the inside trash on Bianca?"

The ground seemed to fall away beneath him. His lungs emptied, and his heart shuddered to a stop. He stared at her. *Make me fall for you.* Her words sliced through his heart, making him realize he'd just lost everything he wanted. Cady. Loving him.

"Well, here's another fact for you. You are an asshole," she snapped, pushing out of his truck and into the shop before he could put together a rational response.

He stared after her, his heart thumping and his chest aching heavily. What was he supposed to do now? Ten seconds ago, it had been crystal clear. Now he wasn't so sure. He didn't want to lose Cady... He swallowed, staring blindly through the windshield.

But he couldn't keep this from Zach. Bianca was making life choices on the opinion of her grandmother and the old woman's dreams—hardly a solid foundation for a long-term commitment. Marriage to someone with commitment issues, regardless of the circumstances, was a bad idea. He ran a hand over his face. What the hell would happen when the old woman dreamed Zach was no good? Would Bianca dump him? His brain was working overtime when Zach came striding out of the flower shop, heading straight to Patton's window.

He glanced at Patton through the glass, his face lined with concern. Patton rolled down the window. "Hey."

"Hey?" Zach asked, shaking his head. "Cady's all bent out of shape."

"Get in," Patton nodded at the passenger door.

"We're kind of in the middle of something. There's not a lot of time to get things pulled together, you know." Zach laughed. "You have a thing for Cady—we all know you two are hot for each other. But your timing sucks—"

"Zach," Patton cut him off. "Did you know Bianca's been engaged before?"

Zach frowned. His jaw tightened before he responded. "You were engaged before. Did you tell Cady? Don't be a dick, Patton—"

"Three times?" Patton finished.

He wasn't sure what was worse, the look on Zach's face or the way his little brother gripped the truck for support. "Three?" He looked at his brother.

"Can you get in the damn truck?" Patton asked again.

"There's more?" Zach was pale.

"Just—"

"No!" Zach yelled back. "I know what you're trying to pull. You want me to call the wedding off? You want me to believe you, without talking to her? Without listening to her side of the story."

Patton's own anger rose. Not at Zach necessarily—but for the whole situation. He didn't want to be the bad guy. He wanted to be the voice of reason. Sometimes the truth hurt, but it didn't change the fact that it was the truth. A truth that had cost him Cady. "Ask her why she broke off the engagements. Ask her about her DWI, too. What else don't you know?" He paused. "I know you care about her, but you need to ask yourself if you know her the way you think you do. Maybe it's better to consider postponing things until then."

Zach was staring at him with such hatred that Patton stopped talking. They'd been so loud that neither of them heard Bianca come out of the shop.

"It's all true." Bianca stood, her hand braced on the handle of the shop door. "I was engaged th-three times. I should have told you. About everything. I'm sorry, Zach." She looked at the ground.

"Why didn't you tell me?" Zach asked, his voice tight and unsteady. "A DWI?"

Bianca shrugged. "I…I was embarrassed." She spoke quickly, her words so soft and rushed it was hard to understand her. "It's not something I'm proud of…something I'd planned. Patton's right."

Zach was staring at her now. "About what?"

Bianca looked at him, the pain in her eyes so intense Patton looked away. "We're rushing this. I think maybe…" Her voice broke. "We need to…to break off our engagement."

Patton felt the weight of her words. His grip tightened on his steering wheel as he looked at his brother. Zach's fists were clenched tightly, his posture so rigid he worried his little brother might just break.

"Don't you think we need to talk?" Zach bit out. "Just the two of us?"

Bianca drew in a deep breath. "Yes… I guess… I don't know, Zach." She sniffed, tears spilling down her cheeks. "Nothing I say can change my past…" She shook her head and wiped her tears away. "It's the right thing to do. We both know it." She cleared her throat, drawing Patton's attention. "So, I'm going to go break the news to my family. You…you should get in touch with your mom before she gets here—so this doesn't get…w-worse."

Zach almost went for her then. Hell, Patton was

tempted, too. But she held her hand up, keeping him at a distance.

"Bianca—" Zach's voice was brittle.

"Please, Zach." Bianca shook her head. "We're all adults here. This isn't the end of the world. Just...us." She disappeared inside her shop.

Zach spun to face him. "I'm sorry your life is shit. But that doesn't mean you need to spread it around." He spun on his heel and walked to the shop. He paused at the door, breathing hard. He stared at the handle, then backed away and headed toward Patton's truck. "I can't deal with Mom right now, but I'm sure you can."

Patton sat there, watching his little brother's truck disappear down the street. He took in a deep breath and picked up his phone.

"What do you need?" Cady asked Bianca for the hundredth time.

Bianca shook her head, her nose swollen and her eyes red and bloodshot. "I can't think. I know there are things that need to get done for work...but I can't wrap my head around it."

Cady pulled her into her arms, her heart broken and aching for her best friend—for herself. "It can wait. Celeste can handle the shop—I can help if she needs anything. Besides, Landon knows what's going on." She pressed a kiss to Bianca's temple.

"I'm so sorry, Cady," Bianca whispered, her voice shaking.

"Why are you apologizing?" she asked. "I'm the one that should be sorry."

"You didn't do anything wrong, Cady," Bianca argued. "You fell in love, you confided, you let go." She sniffed. "And now you've lost him. Like I've lost Zach."

She wanted to argue with Bianca, but there was no way to get the words past the lump in her throat. She hadn't told Bianca about her feelings for Patton or what had happened. There was no need—Bibi knew. She forced herself to argue. "He was never mine, Bibi." The words hurt. "I sure as hell don't want him now."

Bianca pushed out of Cady's hold. "Oh, Cady…" She shook her head. "If things had been reversed, you would have done exactly what Patton did. You would have protected me, no matter what."

Cady scowled at Bianca. Would she? Yes, her allegiance was to Bibi first but… "I would have talked to Zach first. I would have asked him to talk to you. Privately, respectfully—"

"You're you." Bianca shook her head. "They've already lost their brother and their father. Patton's so… guarded. Of course he is going to go straight to Zach."

"I don't want to talk about Patton. Let's focus on you and what will cheer you up." Cady stood, collecting the used tissues that littered the coffee table. "First, I'm making coffee."

"Thank you," Bianca answered. "I'm going to lie here and pull myself together."

Cady smiled at her best friend's sad attempt at a joke. "I think you're holding it together pretty damn well." She paused. "And thank you for not being angry with me."

"I could never be angry with you, Cady. I love you too much," Bianca said with a slow smile.

Guilt hit Cady like a ton of bricks. Would Bibi still feel that way if she'd known about her and Patton's plan?

She hated what had happened today, hated the way it was handled. But today's events had done exactly what she and Patton had wanted. It had ended the engagement—and crushed Bianca.

She'd caught sight of Zach as he stood outside the shop, staring at the door handle. He looked as if he'd been punched—repeatedly—and he hadn't been able to find his bearings. For a moment she hoped he'd come in and talk to Bianca. Anything to make this less horrible. Instead he climbed into his truck and peeled out of the parking lot. Cady was slammed with a wave of self-loathing. What had she been thinking? What right did she have to interfere with Bibi's choice—and her heart?

She'd glared at Patton through the shop window, knowing full well he couldn't see her through the window tinting. It didn't matter. It made her feel better. As much as she blamed herself, she blamed him more.

She made coffee in Bianca's tiny kitchen. The apartment over the shop was minuscule—three "comfy" rooms Bibi called home. It wasn't much, but it was warm and inviting and full of love. Just like Bianca. Cady stared into the coffeepot, her eyes filling with tears.

Today should never have happened. No matter what Bibi said, Cady knew the truth. It was all her fault. If she'd kept her mouth shut, kept Patton at arm's length… She brushed her thoughts aside. What-ifs weren't going to make Bibi feel better. Right now, that was all that mattered.

When she returned with two steaming mugs, heavy on the cream and sugar, she found Bianca poring over a photo album.

Cady sat beside her, smiling at the pictures. "Is that GG?"

"And that handsome devil is my grandfather." Bianca patted the picture. "GG said she still misses him. He's been gone for almost sixteen years."

Cady stared at the picture. There was no denying the young couple in the photograph were deeply in love. "I guess that's real love."

Bianca nodded. "I love how they met. Has GG ever told you the story?" Bianca waited for Cady to shake her head before going on. "They met on a Saturday night; they were both at the cinema with friends and felt that instant thing—you know, that spark? He asked her father for her hand on Wednesday and they were married the following Sunday."

"One week?" Cady was stunned. "And they knew?" She wanted to argue. But she couldn't. She stared at Bianca looking through the album. Bianca had felt that spark with Zach. Cady remembered Bibi's phone call, her friend going on about their instant connection. Cady had downplayed it… Because she hadn't understood. Now, maybe, she did. Love wasn't a choice. She wished she had some way of un-loving Patton, but she couldn't. She hated him for what he did—but she loved him. "You should talk to him, Bibi," Cady spoke, glancing at the phone Bianca had silenced.

Bianca shook her head.

"He's called six times," Cady pushed. "Please call him. Patton might have unloaded a bunch of…facts on him. But you know there's more to the story."

Bianca shrugged. "He'll think better of me if he knows? That he'll still love me?"

Cady nodded. "Of course he will." She swallowed.

She and Bibi had an unspoken promise never to mention her exes, but today she was going to make an exception. "Dan cheated on you so you broke off the engagement. Who wouldn't? Francisco...his accident left you heartbroken. That was why you were driving drunk and got your DWI."

"And Marcus?" Bibi asked.

"You broke it off with him because it didn't feel right, Bibi." Cady sighed. "That doesn't make you a bad person. If anything, it makes you cautious—"

"A cautious person that's been engaged three—four now—times?" Bianca laughed then burst into tears.

"Bibi—"

"Oh." Bianca jumped up, dialing a number. "Yes, yes...This is Bianca Garza...Yes, have you started the alterations on the wedding dress?"

Cady's heart sank lower.

"Oh, good. That's such good news." Bianca paused. "No, no, I won't be purchasing the other dress." Bianca's voice broke.

Cady took the phone and finished the conversation. Bianca didn't need to deal with any of this, not right now. She made arrangements to pick up the dress sometime next week and hung up. Zach tried to call again, but Bianca refused to take his call.

"I want pizza," Bianca said, pulling a quilt over her lap. "And a movie—a comedy. I'd rather laugh than cry."

"Pizza is coming up." Cady nodded. "Find us a movie while I order." She pulled out her phone to order their meal—and tried not to be crushed by the fact that none of her missed calls were from Patton Ryan.

12

CADY SPENT MOST of the weekend at Bianca's. She pulled Bibi out long enough to stock her refrigerator, but Bibi wasn't up for much more. They binge-watched slapstick comedy and ate every variety of takeout. When Bianca needed a cry, Cady let her cry. She didn't know what else to do.

The only good thing that came from the weekend was a smooth program run. She had to login to work a few times to prevent lags, but it hadn't been stressful. Not compared to the rest of the weekend—the rest of her life. Her mind wouldn't stop working. Even when Bianca slept, Cady couldn't. She was worried about Bibi, her family—the Ryans and Zach. Her heart ached for all of them.

Especially Patton.

Bianca's defense had taken some of the bite out of her anger. She was still mad at him for the way he'd handled things, but… Bianca was right. She *would* have told Bibi if things had been reversed… Not that she was willing to forgive and forget. Not yet.

It infuriated her that she was so angry—and yet, she

missed him. But she did. She wanted to see him so she could yell at him. She wanted to fight with him until they'd made peace with what had happened and found a way to make it work. She wanted to touch him… To have him wrap her in his arms. Instead she needed to forget him.

When Cady arrived for work Monday, she was an exhausted train wreck of emotions.

Sadly, the Charles rumor hadn't disappeared. Was he seriously getting her promotion? If she'd been in charge, Charles would have been fired. He was a nice guy, but he was out of his element. He should never—ever—be allowed to write code or touch their security database. Maybe that was his plan? To fail so epically that his father would send him back to the payroll department? Was it possible that—even after the hours of texts, phone calls and meetings, he really hadn't learned a thing from her? When a new error popped up that afternoon, she gave up trying to figure out what he'd done wrong and focused on fixing it. She worked late then crashed on Bibi's couch.

Tuesday she sent her team members a gigantic muffin basket. Sending them on an all-inclusive weekend spa retreat would have been more appropriate, considering how snippy she'd been. But the muffins seemed to do the trick. She worked late on her presentation for the next day's meeting, picked up the wedding dress from the shop and dropped it at Bianca's on the way home. They had dinner and watched some crappy television, but she decided to crash at her own place. Her pillow smelled like Patton, but she couldn't bring herself to wash it. She tossed and turned most of the night.

By Wednesday, she was already ready for the weekend. Instead she was faced with meetings all day. She'd managed to remain calm and positive, even if Charles wouldn't look her in the eye. She introduced a series of trainings she wanted to implement for anyone interested in transferring into coding and her team, to help make things uniform. After the training modules were complete, candidates would test before their request was considered. To her delight, Mr. Hembrecht was in full support.

Cady glanced at the clock. It was only six fifteen, and she was on fumes. She tried to focus, but all she could think about was a bubble bath and a bottle of wine. But before she collapsed into her evening's *entertainment*, she needed to call Bianca and let her know when she was dropping by. They'd exchanged a few texts about going to a late dinner and a pajama screening of some classic horror flick downtown. That would definitely perk Bibi up, if Cady didn't fall asleep first. As the final meeting wound up, she pulled her phone from her purse.

"Cady?" Mr. Hembrecht had waved her over. "Can I have a word?" She smiled, tucked her phone back into her purse and nodded at her boss.

"Are you free for dinner Friday?" he asked. "I have a few things I'd like to discuss with you before the weekend."

Friday night. "Let me check." She scrolled through the planner on her phone. Friday was free. Saturday was supposed to be the bridal shower at Tucker House. She frowned. She needed to take Bibi away—maybe use of some of her vacation time for a girls-only holiday? She smiled at her waiting boss. "Yes. I can do dinner."

"Excellent." He smiled. "Can you walk with me? I

want to hear more on your idea to develop defined user levels for our larger clients' databases."

She followed Mr. Hembrecht back to his office, discussing some of her thoughts on this simple way to streamline and strengthen security. He listened carefully, asking the occasional question now and then. That he was receptive to her idea was heartening, even if it did keep her in the office that much longer.

On her way down the elevator, Meg thanked her—again—for taking her home after the office party and invited her to the gym. "We can burn some calories and pick up some hotties?"

Cady almost turned her down. Almost. But maybe a good workout was just what she needed to shake her restlessness and perk up her energy. "Sure. You can have the hotties."

"Still enjoying being cuffed to your cop, huh?" Meg grinned. "I so don't blame you. Yum."

Cady swallowed down the lump in her throat. "Still involved with that lawyer?"

Meg frowned. "No. Turns out he wasn't as single as he said he was."

Cady frowned. "Ouch. How'd you find out?"

Meg frowned. "I went out to dinner with my sister and saw him at the restaurant. With his wife."

"What did you do?"

Meg shrugged. "I waited until he went to the bathroom, confronted him and left. I didn't have the heart to say anything to his wife." Meg shrugged. "So I'm totally serious about you setting me up with one of Patton's cousins."

"How can you remember that? You were so drunk."

"Um, have you looked at Patton? Of course I'm going

to remember there are men with *that* DNA available—drunk or not."

Cady smiled. "I'll see what I can do."

"Must be nice to date a guy who's so obviously stuck on you." Meg sounded wistful.

She didn't have to worry about Patton being married or cheating on her—because he wasn't hers. She was almost getting used to hurting when she thought about him.

She hit the gym hard. She and Meg parted ways in the parking lot—without a hottie.

Twenty minutes later she was on the side of the road, her car having overheated. So she waited more than an hour before the tow truck came and watched her sports car get pulled away before walking three blocks to a sports bar. She was so hungry she inhaled a burger and some onion rings—getting sucked into the MMA fight on the huge television and drinking way too much before she realized it was getting late. By the time the cab dropped her at her building and she stumbled out of the elevator, she was practically asleep on her feet.

She walked down the hall to find Patton pacing the hall outside her door. His hair was mussed, his shirt rumpled... He looked gorgeous. He froze when he saw her, shoving his hands into his jeans pockets.

"What are you doing here?" she asked, stunned and more than a little excited. Had he been thinking about her? Missing her? Because she had missed him. So much.

"Where have you been?" His gaze was hard, his jaw rigid. He had dark shadows under his eyes and a thick stubble along his jaw. "Bianca said she's been trying to reach you for the last three hours."

As if *he* had any right to be scowling or angry with her. Or hot. So, so hot. "Why are you here?" she asked, wishing she sounded more offended.

"I was picking up the dress from Bianca. She was pretty frantic that she couldn't reach you," he explained, his gaze fixed on her.

Bianca didn't need anything else upsetting her. Poor Bibi… "I didn't get any messages." Cady pulled out her phone. It was dead. She shoved it at him. "I'll call her."

But he was already texting. "She was very upset."

"You said that," she snapped, overwhelmed with disappointment. It shouldn't matter that he'd been sent here. But it did matter. A lot. She'd thought about him far too much since their blowup in the car. Sometimes she'd wanted to yell at him, maybe even pound on his broad chest… But most of the time, she'd hurt. She'd never ached for another person. But Patton made her ache.

Her wants had nothing to do with his visit. He was only here because Bianca had sent him. Not because he wanted to be here—wanted to be with her, to talk to her, to fix things.

His frown grew. "Have you been drinking?"

She narrowed her eyes. *Really?* "Among other things." She didn't need to explain anything to him. She'd had a hell of a week, no thanks to him. And now he was going to show up, teasing her in his tight pants, and drill her with questions? She fished her keys out of her bag, trying to ignore the heat that rolled off him. Or his delectable scent flooding her senses. She would not turn into him, she would not reach out for him. "I'm a young, single adult, Patton," she snapped, unlocking her door and brushing past him into her apartment. "I can do what I want. I sure as hell don't need anyone checking up on me—"

Patton spun her, his hands cupping her cheeks as he kissed her—fiercely, desperately. His mouth parted hers, the stroke of his tongue stealing the air from her lungs. She was vaguely aware of him kicking the door shut as she twined her arms around his neck. Her fingers slid into his hair, pulling him closer. Every inch of her was instantly on fire.

"Cady—" he growled.

This wasn't going to help her get over him. But she needed this—needed him. Her fingers tugged his head forward, drawing his mouth back to hers. His hands gripped her hips, lifting her. She wrapped her legs around him, grinding against him...

They didn't make it to the bedroom.

He was impatient, stripping down to nothing before she'd managed to unbutton the blouse she'd worn to work. She sat on the couch, mesmerized by the raw hunger lining his face. And his amazing body... There was no denying the extent of his need. The sight of him made her ache for him. She reached out, taking the heavy length of his erection in her hand.

He stopped her, his fingers wrapping around her wrist. "I need you." He pulled her up, removing her clothes with a single-minded determination that ratcheted up her hunger. In the back of her mind she knew this was wrong, that this needed to stop before her heart was shredded all over again. But then she was naked and the contact of him, skin on skin, was all that mattered. "Cady... Damn I need you."

She nodded, moaning when he filled her. It was hard and fast. His hands. His mouth. Every thrust. He consumed her and she loved it. She clung to him, gripping his arms as he drove into her. She pressed her lips to his neck, savoring his rough stubble and heady scent. Every nerve, every sense, was flooded with Patton. His fingers brushed over the heated nub between her legs and sent her over the edge. Her release rolled over her, dragging a raw cry from her lips. When they were still breathing heavy, legs and arms tangled together, she looked at him. His eyes were closed, but his face was rigid.

The prick of tears stinging her eyes terrified her. "You should go," she spoke quickly, desperately.

"No, I shouldn't," he argued.

She sat up, away from the comfort of his touch. "I'm too tired for round two." She was, she was exhausted. Not just her body but her heart, too. "You told Bianca I'm okay so—"

"She wasn't the only one worried, Cady. *I* was worried about you." His words were hoarse. "I volunteered to come." He pushed himself up to sit at her side.

She turned to face him, her eyes locking with his. "You did? You were?"

He nodded, pressing his hand to her cheek. "Hell, yes."

His touch was distracting and so were his words. "Mr. Hembrecht asked me to dinner Friday—"

"Why?"

"He wants to discuss work." She paused, but he didn't say anything so she went on. "My car overheated—"

"Why didn't you call me?" he asked, frowning at her.

She shook her head. "It's not your job to take care of me. I take care of myself."

She saw him swallow, saw the slight flare of his nostrils.

"By the time the tow truck got there, I was hungry, so I walked to Chris's for a burger—"

"Best onion rings in town," he interjected. "But you shouldn't be walking around town in the middle of the night, Cady—"

"I ate, had a few beers and watched a few fights." Why was he looking at her like that? "I didn't mean to worry anyone."

"You're okay, that's all that matters."

She was all too vulnerable to this man. Her body hummed with awareness, but her heart was resistant. She couldn't forget that things were different now. And once he left, she would be crushed all over again. "It's late. You need to go."

"Cady, I need to say something." He cleared his throat. "I'm sorry for what happened."

She nodded, fighting the instinct to lean into his hand. "This was apology sex?" she quipped, hoping to defuse the tension.

"This is because I can't keep my hands off you," his voice rumbled, sending chills along her already supersensitive skin.

"We'll have to work on that."

He looked at her for a long time, his gaze exploring every inch of her face. "I'm sorry. I was trying to do what was best for them, for all of us." He shook his head. "Turns out I don't know shit. Zach is at Bianca's right now. I made him come with me to pick up the dress."

"Why?" she asked, stunned.

"She wouldn't answer his calls. And they need to talk." He stroked her cheek again, leaving a trail of fire. "I apologized to Bianca. Now I'm apologizing to you—for hurting you and jeopardizing your friendship."

She stood up, wrapping herself in the throw draped over the back of the couch. She needed distance between them so she could keep a clear mind. "I trusted you. I don't do that easily," she managed. "But I forgive you. I know you love your brother and want what's best for him. Even if I no longer agree with what we did." She paused. "Did you know GG married her husband a week after meeting him?"

He shook his head, his eyes searching hers.

"Next to that, Zach and Bianca's engagement doesn't seem so rushed," she murmured. Her family might not understand what love and commitment meant, but she was beginning to. It didn't matter where she was, in the boardroom or staring at her computer screen, Patton was always on her mind. She wanted him safe. She wanted him happy. Even if he didn't love her. If this was what Bianca felt—what Zach felt—she wasn't going to stop them. She drew in a wavering breath. "So maybe it's possible?"

"That they love each other?" His voice was gruff.

She knew it was possible. It had to be, how else could she feel this way? She loved Patton completely. As scary as that was, it was true. "I…I won't deprive them of happiness. If they decide they want to go through with it, I'll support them."

He nodded. "Okay."

She blinked, waiting. "Just like that?"

"Zach is different with her. I've never seen him so eager to please someone else—and be so damn happy about it. Seeing him this last week, so lost and hurting… I think he does love her. If he's willing to take that chance, I'll be happy for him. And I'll have no problem reminding him of that if there's ever a need." He paused, shaking his head.

She knew he meant it, too. He had a protective streak that would include Bianca once she was family. "Who knew underneath all these hard muscles and tough attitude was a true romantic?"

"Guess this whole experience has made me see things differently." He stood in front of her, making the air spark.

"Differently bad or differently good?" she asked.

His eyes nailed hers, spearing her heart with the intensity of his gaze. "Good. Definitely good," he whispered.

She waited, longing for some sign that *she* might be what he liked, too. That she might be something he'd take a chance on. As great as it was that he was willing to give Bianca and Zach a chance, she wanted more. Never in her life had she imagined she'd want what Bianca did. Not that she'd ever give up her career, it was too much a part of who she was. But with Patton, the house, the companionship, the dog—even the kids— were starting to sound appealing.

"You should go," she said again. "Thanks for checking in on me. And the sex. It was fun."

"Cady—" He frowned, a mix of sadness and frustration in his voice.

"I've got a lot of work before I can go to sleep," she lied, needing him to go.

"Okay," he relented. "I'll see you again?"

"Maybe." She shrugged, trying to act like her world wasn't falling apart.

He tugged his clothes back in place and pulled her

against him. She didn't melt against him, she was proud
of that. She stayed stiff and rigid in his arms. When he
let her go, she smiled but didn't make eye contact. She
locked the door behind him, turned off the lights and
collected her clothes before heading to her bedroom.

Then Cady stood under the shower and cried.

13

CADY STRAIGHTENED ONE of the bows on the back of the chair. Everything looked perfect, almost magazine-worthy really. Bianca and Zach had been lucky Mrs. Ryan had managed to get the library that Saturday at Tucker House for the wedding shower. Considering they'd had only two days, it was amazing how everything had come together so perfectly. The library was smaller than the sunroom they'd originally booked, but no one seemed to mind. Cady preferred this room. With its massive floor-to-ceiling casement windows and a glorious view of the lake, the setting was already lovely.

She and Celeste had been working since the early hours of the morning, setting up tables and chairs, draping tables in peach cloth and arranging countless flower arrangements. Cady had never been much of a do-it-yourself kind of woman, but Bibi was determined to keep their costs at a minimum. And that included decorations. Sure, she'd burned two fingers with a hot-glue gun and sliced her palm with some wired ribbon, but the battle wounds were worth the effort. The room screamed romance.

She smiled as she assessed the space. As much as she'd fought against it, her best friend was getting married in two weeks. And she was going to be the most enthusiastic maid-of-honor-cheerleader ever. Bianca deserved nothing less.

"You two are amazing." Bianca's hazel eyes took in every detail.

"We *are* good." Cady hugged Bianca. "Seriously, I just did what Celeste told me to do. This was totally her vision."

"I'm trying to convince Cady to change careers," Celeste said, nudging Cady in the side.

"So you can expand into wedding planning and parties?" Bianca nodded. "It will happen Celeste, I know it will."

Cady's attention wandered to the door. She was going to be fine. She'd be better if she stopped looking for Patton. He would be here. And she needed to get a grip. If she was lucky, no one but Bianca—and Zach since Bianca told him everything—would pick up on the fact that she was crazy in love with him.

"We've got you set up in the front," Celeste said. "You have the gift registry list, Cady?"

Cady snapped to attention. "Yep, we're ready." She led Bianca to the front of the room.

"You holding up okay?" Bianca whispered.

"I'm fantastic," Cady answered immediately, winking.

Bianca rolled her eyes and took her seat. "You don't have to pretend you're fantastic, Cady. I know you're hurting."

Cady wrinkled her nose. "Who, me? I'm fine," she teased. Yes, she was hurting. But it would go away, she knew that. She had to be strong. She had to resist the pull between them and keep her hands to herself. Seeing him would be hard, but she was going to put her best foot forward—for Bianca and Zach.

Instead of dwelling on Patton's off-limit status, she focused on the party. Bianca should be thrilled over the turnout, especially since it had been called off before it was back on again. Lucy arrived, hugging her before carrying a huge present to the gift table. Cady made small talk with her brothers, Jared and Dean. It really was a shame she couldn't be attracted to Jared... Maybe Meg? She grinned. The idea had potential. At least she knew Jared was single.

Her gaze wandered to the door again. No Patton. It seemed like forever since she'd been wrapped in his arms. Had it really only been three days? So much had happened since she'd seen him last.

Bianca and Zach had reconciled and were going ahead with the wedding. They'd lost their spot at the gardens, but Zach's company had come through in a big way. They were pulling out the stops for him and Bianca and allowing them to use a luxury resort they managed—for a fraction of the cost.

And her dinner with Mr. Hembrecht had made all of her dreams come true.

Except for Patton. He was the only piece of the puzzle that was missing. And she felt it—a huge hole in her heart.

"You look great." Spence hugged her. "How's it going?"

"You looking spiffy yourself." Cady shook her head. "I think it's going well. They look happy and that's what counts." She nodded at the bride- and groom-to-be.

"Yep, they look sickeningly happy," he agreed, making her laugh.

"Cady, Cady, Cady." Mrs. Ryan drew her into a long hug. Then she held her at arm's length. The older woman was all smiles as she said, "I can't tell you how happy I am to see you."

Cady hugged her, casting a curious gaze at Spence—who was trying not to laugh.

"You look so pretty," she paused, glancing at Spence. "Doesn't she, Spence? Such a lovely girl."

"Thank you," Cady murmured, uneasy. Why was Mrs. Ryan looking at her like that? As if she had a secret?

"Come on, Mom, let's go find your daughter-in-law-to-be." Spence steered Mrs. Ryan into the room, leaving Cady to wonder what that was all about.

Cady was straightening presents when the cake was wheeled into the room. A huge pink-and-blue cake, decorated with a massive sugar stork and marshmallow fluff diapers. A hard knot of panic landed heavily in the pit of her stomach. It was the baby-shower-sabotage cake, not the bridal shower cake with lacy frosting and edible pearls. And it was her fault. In all the confusion she'd forgotten to call the bakery and switch the cakes... She moved as quickly as she could, putting herself between the cake and the room full of people.

"There's been a mistake," she said to the young woman pushing the cart. "This can't be right—" But the cart caught on the edge of the area rug, bringing it to a stop—but not the cake. The cake slid forward, splatting the front of Cady's dress.

"Oh, no," the young woman squeaked, covering her mouth with her hands. "I'm so sorry."

Cady looked down at her pale blue-and-white dress... and the smear of bright pink frosting that ran across her stomach and chest.

"Cady?" Mrs. Ryan was up in an instant. "Oh, darling girl, what a mess. You'll need to get club soda on that right—"

"Oh, Cady, your pretty dress," GG said.

She turned to see pure shock on their faces.

"What happened?" Bianca joined the group.

Cady stood—icing sliding down her dress—knowing every pair of eyes in the room was on her. And the cake. The horrible pink-and-blue baby shower cake she'd ordered...

"Is this from Diandra's bakery?" GG recovered first. "Does she know it's a wedding shower? Not a baby shower? That girl was never very bright."

"What's with the huddle?" Spence's eyes widened as he stared at the cake then her dress. "I'll get this back into the kitchen and we'll see about cleaning up this mess."

Zach stepped in. "Spot cleaner? Hose? Napkin?"

Everyone seemed to react at once. Napkins appeared, someone tracked down the front-desk attendant and some spot cleaner. Cady stood there, waiting. No one blew up or jumped to conclusions.

"You are not using Diandra for your wedding cake," GG declared.

Zach was all smiles. "I'll call our number two."

Cady started to laugh then—she had to. She was wound so tight it was laugh or cry. And there was no way she was going to fall apart in front of a room full of people.

The cake cart was on the way back to the kitchen

when she saw Patton. He walked across the room, pausing to take in Cady, the cake explosion and the growing pile of napkins and tissues as her feet. "The bakery called. Something about a mistake and switching the cakes." He held out the large box he was carrying.

But Cady didn't give a damn about the box. Seeing him in a sharp gray suit and light blue shirt, she knew her off-limits plan was in serious jeopardy.

"I don't think we can take this one back," Zach quipped. "Cady's wearing most of it."

Everyone laughed. She tried to laugh.

"Cady?" Bianca asked softly.

She tore her gaze from Patton's, her voice unsteady as she answered, "Hey. At least you get the cake you wanted. My dress was sacrificed for a worthy cause."

"Oh, Cady." Bianca laughed.

"I can get this." Cady took the rag from Bianca. "Go be the bride-to-be. I'm going to find a bathroom." She waved Bianca to her seat and headed to the back. But Patton stood in front of her, blocking her path and sending her heart into overdrive.

Locking eyes with her, he said, "Looks like you dove in front of the cake."

"Um, yes, I did. I guess I panicked." She couldn't stop looking at him. "Did they really call you? Or are you just that good?"

He stared down at her, the corner of his mouth quirking up. "You should know the answer to that."

And just like that, she was aching.

"You look good in pink." His eyes swept over her. "But you look good in anything."

His words warmed her. "I hate pink." She stared down at the stain. "It was a pretty dress."

He laughed.

She couldn't help but smile then.

He smiled, but his gaze remained restless…searching. "I was going to call last night, but work kept me late and I didn't want to wake you." He offered her a glass of punch.

"Thank you." She accepted the glass. His fingers brushed hers, eliciting all sorts of shivers and memories.

He stared at her hand, hard, his jaw clenching.

She took a slow breath. "You were going to call?"

"Dinner? With Hembrecht?" His voice was gravel, his gaze slamming into hers. "How'd it go?"

"Really well." She smiled. He remembered. "He—"

"I think we're about to open the mountain of presents," Zach interrupted, joining them. "Sorry if you get a hand cramp."

"Right, duty calls," she said, glancing at Patton again. He was still staring at her. And it wasn't as if he was trying to hide it. No, he looked at her as if…she was his. And it made her heart go crazy and her lungs desperate for air.

He nodded, his sudden smile so gorgeous she hesitated. She heard Zach's "Take it down a little, Patton. This is a family event," as she made her way to Bianca's side. She couldn't hold back the smile. At least he still wanted her. Too bad that wasn't enough anymore.

She shoved thoughts of Patton and her disappointed heart aside. It was easy to get caught up in the excitement. Bianca was delighted, praising each and every gift and offering thanks the only way Bianca knew how—with hugs. Time and again, Cady sought out Patton. He seemed to be waiting for her, his smile warm and his gaze unwavering. If only she knew what he was thinking.

As the presents piled up, Cady listed every item and who it was from. She made little notes to help keep things straight, check duplicates and possible exchanges or returns. Like the very large glass pelican statue. Who wanted a large glass pelican statue?

She tried to keep her expression neutral, but when she saw Patton's mystified expression, she couldn't stop her giggle. He shook his head, his eyes lingering on her mouth. Even across the room, she felt the heat in his gaze.

It didn't seem to matter that the room was full. Or that Bianca and Lucy and who knew who else was watching them... All that mattered was the way she felt, the hope his attention gave her. She didn't know exactly how she was going to do it but, before the day was through, Patton Ryan was going to know how she felt about him.

"KEEP STARING, I'm not sure the old guy in the corner knows you and Cady are a thing." Spence leaned against the wall beside him. "Nope, wait, I think he's got it, too. Since you two can't stop making eyes at each other."

A thing? Patton grinned. He preferred the term *couple*. Or she was his. But she wasn't, not officially, not yet. He sure as hell hoped she'd be agreeable to the idea.

"I never thought I'd see *you* grinning like a teenager," Spence teased.

Patton glanced at his brother. "Jealous?"

"Maybe," Spence said. "Starting to feel like the odd man out. First Zach and Bianca, now you and Cady. Not that I'm in a hurry to humiliate myself by drooling in public—like you."

Patton ignored his brother, his attention returning

to Cady. She was left-handed, one of the many things he didn't know about her. He used to think of that as a bad thing. Now he knew it meant he had a lot to look forward to. He wouldn't learn everything overnight— it would take years. He hoped it would. He looked forward to each and every one of them.

He slid his hand into his pocket, rubbing the ring inside. As far as rings went, it wasn't too over-the-top. A sizable square-cut diamond solitaire. But, to him, it made a clear statement—a statement he wanted on Cady's hand.

Eventually, the presents turned into cards. He'd put his on the bottom of the stack on purpose. Patton knew it the moment Bianca opened it.

"Patton?" Bianca looked at him. "Cady?" Her eyes filled with tears. "You…you shouldn't have."

Bianca launched herself at Cady, wrapping her arms around Cady and sobbing against her neck. Bianca stood and ran across the room, hugging him and kissing his cheek.

He hugged her back, trying to stay unaffected by her outburst. "Cady said the dress was perfect so… it's yours."

"You have a big heart…" Bianca looked back at Cady. "Both of you."

He looked at Cady, too, but she was staring at the card.

"What did Patton do now?" Zach asked.

Bianca explained, her voice shaking with excitement. "He and Cady bought my wedding dress… My dream dress. The one in the shop that I couldn't really afford."

Patton preferred to stay in the background, but it seemed as if everyone felt the need to hug him, shake his hand or tell him how generous and thoughtful he and Cady were. He remained civil—he hoped.

"Time for cake," Celeste announced, pulling the attention away from him and back to the happy couple. He drew in a deep breath, his gaze sweeping the room for Cady—

"Did you forget to tell me something?" Cady asked, at his side—staring up at him with warm brown eyes.

He stared right back. "We bought Bianca her dress—"

Then she was kissing him, on the lips, in the middle of the room—surrounded by everyone. His arms wrapped around her without thought. She was where she belonged, and he was fine with everyone knowing it.

He lifted his head, smiling down at her. She looked so beautiful…he couldn't wait. He took her hand in his and pulled her from the room and out of the inn. He didn't stop until they were alone. It was a beautiful spring day, a cool breeze blowing a large wicker swing on the inn's wraparound porch. But all he could see was Cady.

He kissed her then, softly, his eyes searching hers.

"Patton," she said softly. "What am I going to do with you?"

"I have a few ideas," he answered, pressing another kiss to her lips. His nerves were shot, but he knew what he had to do.

"Why didn't you tell me?" she asked.

"I wanted to surprise you."

"Me?" she asked, a small smile on her face.

"I wanted Bianca to have the dress she wanted, don't get me wrong. But I knew it would make you happy, too." His confession spilled out, leaving his chest heavy…full. "I want to make you happy, Cady."

"You want to make me happy?" she whispered.

He nodded, tucking her hair behind her ear. "You make me happy."

"I do?" Her voice faltered.

He pulled the ring from his pocket and held it up. His heart beat rapidly, every inch of him braced... Hopeful but wary.

Her eyes were wide, flitting back and forth between him and the ring. "What happened to not rushing to the altar?"

"Cady, if I'm marrying you, you can't get me there fast enough," Patton said, laying it all on the line. He knew it was a risk, but she wasn't running yet.

"Really?" Her brown eyes sparkled—and so did her smile.

He swallowed, his nerves on edge. "Marry me."

"Are you asking me? Or telling me?"

He shrugged, needing her answer so he could breathe again. "Whatever it takes."

"Whatever?" she asked, her brow furrowing ever so slightly.

He nodded, his heart in his throat. "I'll keep asking until I get the answer I want."

"Even if I'd rather go the easy route—like city hall? Or a trip to Vegas? Something small—without all the bells and whistles?"

He could breathe again. "So that's a yes?"

"That's a yes." She held her hand out. It was trembling.

He slid the ring on her finger then kissed her hand and placed it on his chest. He stepped closer, winding his arms around her. Now, finally, she was his. "I love you."

"It's about time you said it," she murmured, pressing her lips against his. "I guess this makes me the luckiest woman in the world. First, a promotion—"

Patton leaned back so he could see her. "I knew it."

She nodded. "Charles is heading up HR, which is what he wants. And I'm getting what I want—a big corner office with a fabulous view and a fabulous raise." She kissed him. "And you." She stared up at him, her voice wavering as she added, "More importantly, you." She shook her head. "The fact that you're incredible in bed is an added bonus. See, lucky."

He chuckled. "You work hard, Cady, that's not luck. I'm glad they appreciate you. They should." He pulled her close again. "You deserve it."

"It means a lot that you believe in me, Patton." She pressed her hand to his cheek. "We have to promise, right now, we'll put each other before our careers. I know it'll be hard and require a lot of work, on both our parts, but I want this to work. I want us to work," she said, glancing at the ring on her finger. "I need us to work. I know who I am, I like who I am. But with you, I'm better."

"Agreed." He kissed her hand, her words filling his head and heart. "You're want I want, what I need." His hand cupped her cheek. "I love you."

"I love you, too," she murmured, her brown gaze locking with his. "Guess we should get back to the party now?" She paused, smiling up at him and taking his hand in hers. "Bianca will be so relieved."

"Relieved?" he asked, letting her lead him back inside.

"Her dream," Cady explained. "She had a dream about us."

"Right. The whole matchmaking thing?"

She nodded. "And I guess it's good news for us, too."

Patton quirked an eyebrow. "How so?"

"The Garza women pride themselves on their matches." She stopped walking, standing on tiptoe to kiss him. "Love matches…that last a lifetime."

He drew her into his arms again. "I like the sound of that."

"Me, too," she said between kisses. "Me, too."

Epilogue

"My feet hurt," Cady whispered in Patton's ear.

"I love it when you talk dirty," he answered.

She laughed, staring up at him.

The dance floor was almost deserted now. Bianca and Zach—the bride and groom—had left, the party was winding down and it was time for Cady's surprise.

"Does that mean you're ready to go?" she asked.

"Go?" he asked. "I thought we were staying here tonight?" He gave her a wicked look.

"We are..." She took his hand and tugged him off the dance floor. "But first we're taking a field trip." She didn't stop until they walked out the front doors of the hotel. "If you're up for it?" she asked.

Patton's jaw clenched tightly as he inspected the limo that waited. When he looked at her, she didn't need to hear him say, "Oh, I'm up for it."

The driver opened the door and Cady climbed right in. Patton's hands were on her before the door was shut.

"Tell me about this fantasy, Detective," she whispered, tilting her head back for a kiss.

"How about I show you?" he asked, pressing his

lips to her neck. His hand rested on her thigh, burning through the silk of her bridesmaid dress. When he lifted his head, she twisted her fingers in his hair and tugged his mouth to hers.

The lights from the city outside spilled into the cab, just enough light to see him. And how much he wanted her.

His fingers were quick on the zipper of her dress. The straps slipped off her shoulders and the dress slid down, pooling around her waist. He pulled the skirt up, revealing her thigh-high stockings and garter belt. "Damn, Cady," he murmured, running his fingers along the garter ties. "You're beautiful." He looked at her. His hunger was raw, his control on the edge. But she saw love in his gaze and felt it in her heart. She'd never felt as beautiful, as desired.

"Kiss me," she whispered, leaning into his hands—and his mouth.

He did. His tongue stroked the seam of her lips, asking for more. Her lips parted beneath his, his kiss making her limbs weak and her body throb.

How he managed to remove her panties, she didn't know. One minute she was beside him, the next she straddled him, his head falling back against the seat as he slid deep inside of her.

"I like this fantasy," she whispered, unbuttoning his shirt to touch him.

His hands gripped her hips. "We're just getting started," he promised.

* * * * *

#891 DARING HER SEAL
Uniformly Hot!
by Anne Marsh
DEA agent Ashley Dixon and Navy SEAL Levi Brandon are
shocked to discover their faux wedding from their last mission
was legitimate. They don't even like each other! Which doesn't
mean they aren't hot for each other...

#892 COME CLOSER, COWBOY
Made in Montana
by Debbi Rawlins
Hollywood transplant Mallory Brandt is opening a new bar in
Blackfoot Falls. She needs a fresh start, but sexy stuntman
Gunner Ellison is determined to remind her of the past...one
amazing night in particular.

#893 BIG SKY SEDUCTION
by Daire St. Denis
When uptight Gloria Hurst sleeps with laid-back cowboy
Dillon Cross, she does what any control freak would do—pretend
it never happened. But a moment of weakness is quickly turning
into something that could last a lifetime!

#894 THE FLYBOY'S TEMPTATION
by Kimberly Van Meter
Former Air Force pilot J.T. Carmichael knew Dr. Hope Larsen's
request to fly into the Mexican jungle came with a mess of
complications. But when they're stranded, the heat between
them becomes too hard to resist...

REQUEST YOUR FREE BOOKS!
2 FREE NOVELS PLUS 2 FREE GIFTS!

HARLEQUIN®

Desire

ALWAYS POWERFUL, PASSIONATE AND PROVOCATIVE

YES! Please send me 2 FREE Harlequin® Desire novels and my 2 FREE gifts (gifts are worth about $10). After receiving them, if I don't wish to receive any more books, I can return the shipping statement marked "cancel." If I don't cancel, I will receive 6 brand-new novels every month and be billed just $4.55 per book in the U.S. or $5.24 per book in Canada. That's a savings of at least 13% off the cover price! It's quite a bargain! Shipping and handling is just 50¢ per book in the U.S. and 75¢ per book in Canada.* I understand that accepting the 2 free books and gifts places me under no obligation to buy anything. I can always return a shipment and cancel at any time. Even if I never buy another book, the two free books and gifts are mine to keep forever.

225/326 HDN GH2P

Name _____ (PLEASE PRINT)

Address _____ Apt. #

City _____ State/Prov. _____ Zip/Postal Code

Signature (if under 18, a parent or guardian must sign)

Mail to the **Reader Service:**
IN U.S.A.: P.O. Box 1867, Buffalo, NY 14240-1867
IN CANADA: P.O. Box 609, Fort Erie, Ontario L2A 5X3

Want to try two free books from another line?
Call 1-800-873-8635 or visit www.ReaderService.com.

* Terms and prices subject to change without notice. Prices do not include applicable taxes. Sales tax applicable in N.Y. Canadian residents will be charged applicable taxes. Offer not valid in Quebec. This offer is limited to one order per household. Not valid for current subscribers to Harlequin Desire books. All orders subject to credit approval. Credit or debit balances in a customer's account(s) may be offset by any other outstanding balance owed by or to the customer. Please allow 4 to 6 weeks for delivery. Offer available while quantities last.

Your Privacy—The Reader Service is committed to protecting your privacy. Our Privacy Policy is available online at www.ReaderService.com or upon request from the Reader Service.

We make a portion of our mailing list available to reputable third parties that offer products we believe may interest you. If you prefer that we not exchange your name with third parties, or if you wish to clarify or modify your communication preferences, please visit us at www.ReaderService.com/consumerschoice or write to us at Reader Service Preference Service, P.O. Box 9062, Buffalo, NY 14240-9062. Include your complete name and address.

HD15

"Can you be married without having sex?"

Levi Brandon's SEAL team leader, Gray Jackson, slapped him on the back, harder than was strictly necessary. "Last time I checked, you weren't married, planning on getting married or even dating the same woman for consecutive nights. The better question is... can you go without having sex?"

He'd tried dating when he was younger. Hell. The word *younger* made him feel like Methuselah, but the feeling wasn't inaccurate. Courtesy of Uncle Sam, he'd seen plenty and done more. The civilian women he'd dated once upon a time didn't understand what his job entailed.

He certainly had no plans for celibacy. On the other hand, fate had just slapped him with the moral equivalent of a chastity belt. Levi pulled the marriage certificate out of a pocket of his flight suit and waved it at his team.

Sam unfolded the paper, read it over and whistled. "You're married?"

"Not on purpose," Levi admitted with a scowl.

Mason held out a hand for the certificate. "When did this happen?"

"I'm blaming you." Mason was a big bear of a SEAL, a damned good sniper and the second member of their unit to find *true love* when they'd been undercover on Fantasy Island three months ago. "Your girl asked Ashley and me to be the stand-in bride and groom for a beach ceremony. She didn't tell us we were getting married for real."

Mason grinned. "Heads up. Every photo shoot with that woman is an adventure."

"Yeah," he grumbled, "but can you really imagine me married? To *Ashley*?"

Ashley Dixon had been a DEA tagalong on their past two missions. As far as he could tell, she disliked everything about him—she'd been happy to detail her opinions loudly and at length. Naturally he'd given her plenty of shit while they'd been in their field together, and she'd *really* hated him calling her Mrs. Brandon after they'd played bride and groom for Mason's girl.

After they'd parted ways on Fantasy Island, he hadn't thought of her once. Okay. He'd thought of her once. Maybe twice. She was gorgeous, they had a little history together and he wasn't dead yet, although he was fairly certain he *would* be if he pursued her. But how the hell had he ended up married to her?

Don't miss DARING HER SEAL
by New York Times *bestselling author Anne Marsh,*
available May 2016 wherever
Harlequin® Blaze® books and ebooks are sold.

www.Harlequin.com

Looking for more passionate reads?
Collect these stories from
Harlequin Presents and Harlequin Desire!